Muriel Cerf

STREET GIRL

Translated by Dominic Di Bernardi

The Dalkey Archive Press

Originally published by Mercure de France, 1975
Copyright © 1975 Mercure de France
This translation copyright © 1988 Dominic Di Bernardi
English language copyright © 1988 The Dalkey Archive Press

Library of Congress Cataloging in Publication Data
Cerf, Muriel.
    [*Rois et les voleurs.* English]
    Street Girl / Muriel Cerf: translated by Dominic Di Bernardi.
    Translation of: *Les rois et les voleurs.*
PQ2663.E732R613 1988   843'.914—dc19   88-23694
ISBN: 0-916583-29-5

First Edition

Partially funded by grants from The National Endowment for the Arts and
The Illinois Arts Council.

The Dalkey Archive Press
1817 North 79th Avenue
Elmwood Park, IL 60635 USA

for Jean-José Andrieu

"... the privilege of being at home everywhere like kings, streetwalkers, and thieves."

Balzac, Splendeurs et misères des courtisanes

I

The Horses of Surf

Childhood, land of abysses where Neptune gallops on his horses of surf, mares of the September tides, which wash over the Gois Passage while leaving behind on my fingertips a bit of foam flung from the crest of the waves, a milky effervescence, a siren's saliva, a river where, adrift, I am tossed by the rush of fantasies like those lunatics abandoned in their red ships or Beautiful Elaine in the black bark carrying her far from the land of Astolat.

To Get Childhood Out of the Way

Lydie Tristan. Myself. Yourself. Oneself. A six-month-old baby, flat on its belly upon a crone's stark-naked skin. So awfully like other babies. A surprising feeling of schizophrenia. Oneself and another. Impossible to synchronize the image of this chubby hominid and the one a person gets used to seeing in the mirror. As for a fetal memory—zero. And the fabulous, unique instant when the paternal spermatazoon slips into the maternal ovum dawdling way back somewhere in the ovarian labyrinth—gone forever. And the nine months spent in the tepid cesspool—forgotten. What's left is nostalgia, so they say. What's left is the terrific hodgepodge of gametes, the laws of heredity, the amount of proteins Mommy took in, and splat fetus king of the world comes out like a bloody missile trailing after its filaments of plasma witches' drool and clots of divine snot—it's all over now, the great uterine night and the reassuring knock of the sea inside, here it comes expelled from its membrane paradise, chased from its moist transparent sphere suffused with phosphenes, emerged from the primordial alluvium, condemned to open air, chained for life to its responsibility, and above all forced to bear the burden of this incredible privilege—to be unique in its species, cut off from the universe, ALONE and conscious of being so, as soon as with one guillotine blade-like whack the umbilical cord is burst that was holding it to the roots of the world.

Then comes childhood. The great myth. The Promised Land Lost. And the old folks rambling on how they remember their kiddie Christmases, with turkey, electric trains, and all those things. And going back to school in the fall, the smell of leather bookbags, new erasers, ink on the fingers—the very thought makes them blubber. You get the impression that the years they spent cooped up in lycées, both public and private, boarding schools and other ghettos, contained the only dream and adventure of their entire existence, and still glittered with the satanic sparkle of a spell whose secret had been stolen from them; diploma in hand, there they go flung *intothejobmarket,* bye-bye to the irresponsible goofing around of school years. I see my mother again across the table saying: When the young people of your generation, the postwar kids, are on the point of *enteringthejobmarket* then we'll see if they make out any better than we did, and she licked her chops in advance, picturing these martyrs decked out in a stiff collar like Dad's, sticking their fingers into the machinery meant to mash them up real good. So long live the reservoir of memories, oh-if-only-I-could-have-never-grown-up, stuck my head in the sand until I died so as not to find myself eyeball-to-eyeball with a mess of problems without solution: where is the earth headed, what's going to replace paper and oil and nylon and plastic and butane and diesel and wool, how can a person keep from croaking with a swollen belly because of some polluted fish he gobbled down or keep from drifting out into the middle of an ocean of garbage between sudsy shores of detergents full of enzymes? A sad end indeed for the pride of a Westerner. Thus the demoralizing ditty on the charm of childhood. Only thing is they forgot about the psychoanalysts who, vicious creatures that they are, pounce on this unfortunate fringe of life still left intact, break its cherry for us, mud-splatter it with their tales of castration, frustration, and unresolved Oedipus—what's unfortunate, my angels, is that, even so, they're right.

An affluent childhood—cushy, castrated, and protected —is really one Filthy Mess. Through the prism of my ten years I see life again as it appeared to me back then, an old doddering Petainist auntie with drool on her chin. The earth, an enormous old folks' home. School, or rather the private Academy, something like quarantine. Plus, hell (i.e., other people), all those daughters of furriers and diamond merchants in the neighborhood who preferred to fork over rather than allow their little blonde angels to brush shoulders with the plebs in the local grade school. So then, the S— Academy, way back in a blackish street more mud-splattered, more gray with pigeon droppings, more drenched with dog piss than an alley in Katmandou running with manure, at one end rue La Fayette, on the other the Folies-Bergères and Faubourg-Montmartre, a trap-infested jungle, the North Africans' turf, fief of the Béberts and Arons sons of Tunis, kingdom of pustule and smallpox steeped in the smoke from chestnuts and fried dough, paradise of vice crammed with three-franc movie houses, oriental bakeries and hair salons stinking of Roja brilliantine, a seedy, lecherous, dank, low-life, smutty universe that allowed me to surmise that, behind the sterilized appearances of the life that was shown to me, there existed another sort, with dazzling colors and suffocating smells, a life of head-spinning thrills and forbidden games. So we would stuff our faces on the sly with pistachios and coconut Turkish delights in one of the small Arab cafés in the Faubourg, we would cut classes and go take up our places in front of the tube to ogle Ivanhoe's beefy biceps, we would fill up our

lungs with gasoline as if it were iodized air, We meaning Me
at the head of the class, the cross on the lapel of my navy
blue blazer making me about as happy as the Legion of
Honor medal would a Leftist, me Lydie, pretty little girl
made out of sugar, or porcelain, for a few hours of hookey
forgetting the jealousies, spites, Low Masses and poisonous
nastiness of the girls in my class, pacing up and down the
Faubourg like a caged lion while furiously licking the twist
of a pistachio ice cream in the company of Cassinoux, my
one and only girlfriend, the first in a series of Girlfriends and
the last in the class, with a mustache, a stutter and a lisp all at
the same time, who dragged along in her wake all the old
men strolling about the area, fascinated by the regular
swaying movement of the remarkable waltzing boy inso-
lently snug in his pleated schoolgirl's skirt.

Until the age of twelve, life was a nightmare. Schizophrenia off to a nice start. The world around me was
padded, muffled, bland and echoless. I could kick at the
door with all my strength, but nobody gave the impression
of wanting to pull me out of this dreadful soundproof
prison. In my kiddie microsociety, I was learning that
human beings were nasty and aggressive; beginning in
fourth grade I would discover, special thanks to my math
teacher, that they were also weak, masochistic, spineless,
gregarious, passive, always ready to side with the strongest,
greedy for fresh blood and human flesh. Math class was a
three-ring circus. *Panem et circenses.* No sooner would
Madame Benazouli, whom I can't ever remember seeing
when she wasn't pregnant, walk into the class, thrusting out
before her the arrogant protuberance of a stomach destined
to become monstrous by the end of the school year, than a
gust of panic would flatten every head, we would lower our
noses, hunch our necks down into our shoulders, arch our
backs, camouflage ourselves in our mental shells awaiting

the moment we would find out who, today, would be eaten up alive, skinned by hand, sliced up into thin transparent strips (that is, go up to the blackboard for the oral quiz). Benazouli would settle herself in with a calculated slowness, skillfully interposing her belly between the chair and desk as if it were some kind of fragile hot air balloon that had a life apart from her own; she would open the rollbook without releasing us from the opaque stare of her huge fly-eyes, glazed and restless, and she would begin to call out our names; when she got to Zabrovsky, the whole class was practically congealed in its juice, fixed in the silence of an icy planet, gasping for breath in an atmosphere as thin as a submarine's subjected to deep-water pressure; then her pencil would rise to the top of the list, followed by twenty pairs of stupefied eyes, and it would begin its hellish waltz, hesitating, gyrating, skipping lines, before landing point-first, pop, upon . . . PLOT! up at the blackboard! Poor old Plot, Angèle Plot, slowly drew near the rostrum with the hypnotic stare of a chameleon caught in the act of turning red against green. Benazouli fixed her prey for a moment with a satisfied smile, caressing the ruler she rapped our fingers with, and she began questioning in a syrupy voice while mechanically touching her thyroid, an organ whose prominence was responsible for all kinds of glandular problems, like the way her eyes bulged from their sockets, their bilious green color rivaling her gallbladder's, which had been making her life constantly miserable from the start of her permanent pregnancies. So then, while Benazouli was stroking a thyroid as pointy as a prehistoric lizard's stinger while holding back the vague bittersweetness of a sugary nausea, Plot erased the blackboard with broad sweeps of a dry sponge that eventually started to creak, krrr . . . PLOT YOU DUMBBELL CAN'T YOU GO WET THE SPONGE, Benazouli hollered, her teeth on edge and her gallbladder convulsing with horror—from that moment on, Plot might well solve the most Machiavellian problems dealing with trains and faucets, but no matter what, she was a goner, and knowing this, her fear made her hunch her neck, all one inch of it, down into her shoulders, thus transforming her into a caryatid, a woman trunk, a cylinder, a geometrical fish gasping air through its minuscule gills, a human machine stopped dead, a disconnected metabolism, only living by the piss of terror she started trickling into her Bateau panties the second she saw Benazouli come forward, a green dragon with wings spread wide, steel claws raised upon her, spitting fire and ready to burn her lungs with the vehement lashes of her incandescent tongue.

But the worst thing was that the whole class approved. Never would anybody have thought to question the right of life and death the teacher had over her pupils. She might just as well have killed one of them, leapt onto her stomach, and spun her guts out around her head like a turban and not once would the frozen, distressed, respectful silence have been disturbed in the slightest. Her big specialty was slaps, and not simple friendly pats either, but round-trip deliveries that would send us reeling into the stove on the other side of the blackboard. And we—by that I mean *me* and my retarded girlfriend Cassinoux, that exquisite dumbbell on the brink of autism who drooled on her copybooks—we found that normal, in any case legal, with the curious masochism of kids terrified before a world governed by a system of rules as implacable and intangible as those the magi of Sumer inscribed on their basalt tablets. I'd even go so far as to say that if most of them kept track of the ruckus with a glum, resigned gaze, some actually giggled at Benazouli's cruel jibes, displaying a terrorized admiration for her that struck me as the depths of abjection; just one more step and they would have licked her shoes, those traitors, those collaborators, without forgetting the muck stuck to the soles.

Under Benazouli's dress, day by day, an obscene ball was swelling up that pulled the pleats almost horizontal, and I, fascinated, imagined her in the buff, all scrawny, bulging at the waist with this blister, this translucent sack, this hump that made her look like a python with a stomach stuffed by a mountain cub; I tried to pierce through appearances beyond the dress and skin, to strip her to her most intimate regions; I would have loved to peel her like an onion to reach the vital place where the heart of the hydrocephalic monster denting her belly with its fits of rage was supposed to be beating. I absorbed myself in a feverish exercise of mental concentration to telepathically capture the diabolical baby's attention—go to it, I would say, bite her, pinch her, scratch her, kick her guts in, let her have it with the left, there, way to go, bang, pow—while all around me wide-open faucets were streaming with green bile and mad trains driven by Benazouli, eyes popping out of her head and her thyroid jumping about, charged full blast along rails to which she had roped us beforehand, side by side all in a row.

*

Still dazed by the whistling of the V2s, the Young Couples of the postwar entered a brand-new world, the world of peace that was theirs to conquer, with frenetic good intentions that first of all bore down on what came out of their bellies: children. That's where Poppa Freud stepped in. If they hadn't really read Freud, they came up with a general idea, from which they drew the conclusion that subduing children with a lash of a whip, a technique so close to the hearts of the previous generation, had to be replaced by skillful, subtle, and meticulous training. For the first time people turned their attention upon this nebulous fringe of an individual's life: the first years, Childhood Concept, a world imagined, normalized, reconstructed by adults too far from their own memories for this magical edifice to bear any relationship to reality. And then began the tragedy of Good Intentions.

Provided with guilt complexes in advance—every upbringing is basically a failure, Doctor Freud said—frozen in their feeling of permanent responsibility (was I right to refuse the child an ice cream bar, to send her to summer camp, to enroll her in a private school?) mothers, those formidable beasts of burden, made themselves absolutely miserable fussing over, dolling up, and protecting from rain and shine poor seven-year-old rhesus monkeys who asked for one thing only: to escape now and then the attention of an anxious family circle which JUDGED and INTERPRETED their slightest gesture according to the dictates of a predigested psychoanalysis. Impossible to escape Mommy's severe and affectionate gaze following them right onto the toilet, into the back of storage closets, behind school walls, under park benches, a look of love as ineluctable as the Buddha painted on the golden cubes of Nepalese stupas, as the gaze in seventeenth-century Flemish portraits, where, no matter where you stand, the burgermaster's pupil, slipping over the cornea, tracks you through the centuries with its methodical attention.

But let's get back to where we started. This was the beginning of mummification and metamorphosis. In order to maintain an outward look suitable for the children of the living dead, their bowels were yanked out through their noses, their intestines emptied, they were disinfected with myrrh and cinnamon, had their tummies stuffed with sawdust and resewn, and they were left to steep in a natron bath perfumed with rare essences so that they wouldn't be offended by the smell of their own bodies, after which they were bound with silk strips, penis and clitoris having been razored off, their mouths were gagged with gold paint, they were stuck in the middle of a superb pyramid, the torches were put out, and they remained undisturbed for twenty-one years of darkness with the words: It serves them right.

By luck I escaped mummification, that is, twelve years of boarding school, in order to undergo the second process: metamorphosis. So I was turned into a childlike K., into a cockroach, and my distress ranked right alongside the unfortunate creature's up on the ceiling and suffocating in his shell—all I had to do was wait for the day when this ridiculous disguise, coming apart at every seam, would be removed so I would finally look like what I was: a being of the resolutely feminine sex, all sparkling, all bouncy, all frisky, ready to charge into the world and delighted by the view of the twenty-first century, a paradisical vision of myself that had nothing in common, alas, with what's called reality, the image that mirrors reflect when they lack the sparkle of wit and other people's eyes which even more rarely show some sparkle, the image of an insect with the dull, dirty color of fleas, bedbugs and cockroaches, a wall color that gave me this hated privilege: invisibility. I blended into the floor, the furniture, the ceiling. They thought I was on the table and I was under the bureau. For twelve years I lived through the metamorphosed soul's nightmare, Ulysses' mates squealing in their pig flesh and slopping around in Circe's trough, Merlin turned into an old man by Vivien, etc.

I was turned into an infant, an alienating condition that I refused with stamping feet, then into a little girl—at that point I didn't even have the energy left to kick up a fuss. I was depersonalized, dissociated, in bits and pieces, scattered, blurry, evanescent, a shadow of my double parodying my role, unable to put the pieces of my puzzle together again in order to take action. Imagine waking up one morning and, instead of catching sight of your familiar reflection in the mirror, you find yourself faced with a Colorado beetle, a bedbug, or a bluebottle fly; imagine that you're a transsexual who feels that he is all woman to his fingertips and knows himself to be a man with beard, mustache, and all the attributes of a superficial virility that he must somehow live with. My transvestite drag was my bedbug shape. What's more, I saw myself living, washing, breathing, eating with a merciless distant eye, constantly turning myself into an object, jealous of the people around me who executed daily movements and reflexes with the certainty of automatons and in whom the motor impulse was communicated with an electrical current's speed to the far tips of their nerve ends, thus allowing them to carry out actions without a hitch, whereas just lifting my pinky or brushing my hair demanded a Dantean effort from me. Before undertaking anything at all, I would judge it, meaning, I would size it up; I circled it like a toreador before a bull, vainly shaking my ridiculous cape, before fleeing in despair in front of the booing crowd, seized by an uncontrollable cosmic laughter—the famous horrible laughter that called into question the life of Camus's penitent judge when he heard it for the first time while strolling on the quays of the Seine; I made a promise to myself that one day, when my crappy self would have defined its limits, I would win the ears and tail of this damned bull, but already the arena was emptying out while, crazy with powerlessness, I heard magnified into the heavens the rending echo of universal derision.

*

Everything is permitted regarding children. At ten you can feel yourself to be Venus and Michelangelo at the same time, and still see yourself ordered to finish your spinach and shut your trap under threat of jail. But there are other vexations. When I turned eight my mother had bought me, along with the Ben Hur game and the indispensable Monopoly, the complete collection of the "World of Knowledge" series. A prodigious name. The world came suddenly into my possession with the help of an illustrated encyclopedia —arts, sciences, history, discoveries, legends and other educational documents. On the first page the planetary globe "blue as an orange," wrapped in a ribbon of paper upon which an Eskimo was watching a royal galley sail off into the distance while a Komodo dragon hoisted itself onto a shore where a falcon was battling a snake. Merely scanning the table of contents made my mouth water. Amerigo Vespucci was followed by Brocades, and all jumbled up: Banana, Batracian, Blood, Crickets, Gallinacean, Leonardo da Vinci, Nobel Alfred, Phosphorescent Rain, Pinocchio, Saliva, Tobacco and Truffles. With the World of Knowledge, I straddled comets to follow their ellipses around the sun, charging head down onto the orbit of Perseus with my flaming rocket squeezed between my thighs, hanging on with all my might to the nucleus, my fingers clinging to the slender mane of the meteors; I learned with polite interest that bees with fine palates preferred the nectar of red clover and heather to that of other flowers, that butterflies have their hearts and stomachs in their backs and that the potato was introduced into Italy by the barefooted Carmelites; I strolled through the hypostyle of the Temple of Karnak between columns with their capitals mysteriously opened or closed; I slept guarded by the four faces of Isis. I was received at the court of Sargon and of Persepolis before its ruins got to looking like a burned-down forest; I danced before the ark in Solomon's Temple; I poked my nose through the propylaea all over the Acropolis; my backside planted on the ruins of Carthage, I meditated with Marius defeated by Sylla upon the fragility of men and empires; I dived to the bottom of the ocean between forests of petrified coral to pry oysters from the rock; I learned about life on the moon and the death of pearls; I skirted the South Pole on Cook's ships; I followed the procession of caterpillars (sometimes as many as three hundred) charging up tall pines; I flitted above fields with the pieridaen butterfly, above jungles with the *Ornithoptera paradisea* (New Guinea), and upon magnolias with the Madagascar chrysalis; I deposited my eggs in clumps beside the plum moth's —but I preferred the crepuscular butterflies, like the *actias luna,* that Chinese kite with long wings stamped with the seal of the moon—and I was in ecstasy over the nebulous forms of living cells, especially chicken monocytes.

But my mother, in her doctrinaire naiveté, did not mean for me to gobble down all this encyclopedic fodder so blindly, knowledge quite often being the seed of evil, so she diligently checked all the permitted articles with a blue pencil and those off-limits with a red ballpoint; for example, the chapter on the reproduction of fucus, which might have put ideas into my head. Now, having ideas was the very least of my problems; I'd even go so far as to say that I suffered from a sheer excess poured out in the form of literary reflections in the style of Théophile Gautier on his Chinese enamels. At the age of five I undertook my great project, a history of ants as interminable as their fearsome, monomaniacal march (they were red ants, naturally) with accompanying illustrations (ants stretching for miles); at eight I threw myself into a series of adventures in the taiga, and at ten I had rewritten in comic-strip form the *Iliad,* the *Odyssey,* the Arthurian legends and *The Jungle Book,* a considerable labor that plunged my family into a state of dumbfounded fascination. I looked and I read, then I drew and I wrote, a digestive mechanism as regular as the Yorkshire's which, no sooner its mishmash gulped down, rushes to transform it in the middle of the sidewalk in the shape of a sorry-looking blood sausage that generally sets the dog's owner marveling. Let creators continue to envelop the whole process in an Olympian mystery and let the Goncourts veil their faces; for me it's been the same thing ever since I was five, and a person's got to be soft in the head to make so much flap about a printed thing. Whether it's molten lead transformed into gold by way of a weird neuronic alchemy, or pigeon droppings—same process, same result. Ditto for collecting the divine droppings and putting them in a shovel and burning them at the foot of the God of Writing. Okay, fine. Now, to get back to my Childhood Concept, to this dungeon where I had been splashing around so long that I had forgotten that outside and above there was the sky and the marvelous clouds. What I didn't know in my distress and in the deepest depths of my boredom was that I wasn't the only one in my situation. Hundreds of scared little kids were trapped in the same way, their necks in Mommy's stranglehold, hiccuping, desperate for air to breathe, twisting and turning like harpooned whales, striking out with their fearsome tails to race off through the waves to rejoin their fellow creatures and to leap in scorn and flout from a distance the enemy left behind on the shore. To continue my treasured comparisons with the animal world—a fabulous world of purity, essence, and instinct—thousands

of kids born after the war squirming in their traps swore that
one day they would get out to lead a real life, the life of foxes
in the woods, vulpine braggarts who steal to live and dash
through the adventurous forest, although it may mean
leaving behind some fur, some teeth, a bit of ear, who fly like
the wind, muzzles stretched forward, eyes alert, paws
grazed (but who cares?), ears whistling with the barking of
the dogs hot on their trail.

But Polline and I—Polline, here she is already at the tip of
my pen—we were going to organize for ourselves a genuine
wild-animal refuge dedicated to fighting tooth and nail and
beak and claw and paw and tail, charging, biting, slavering,
growling, meowing, barking and neighing—God when I
think about it, what absolute happiness it is knowing whom
and what to fight against, something really rigid, really solid,
really opaque, that's named Barrier, Prohibition, Morality, a
Filthy Mess or anything you want—no risk of turning your
weapons upon yourself in such situations and battling your
own demons, no way; there things were simple, life was
forbidden to us and we didn't want to die, so we had to
charge ahead, join forces, wage war, what else? The eternal
game, titillatingly dirty and cruel. Shut up, you don't know
what life's really like, my mother says. If you knew, you
wouldn't talk like that. I would have wound up as a resister
or a collaborator just so I could go all the way. But the war
we had on our hands was against a Louis-Phillipoid
nineteenth century grown fat and sluggish on rotgut wine,
and not really a war either, but rather a revolution.

Oneiroland

Twelve years sealed with a sickly sweet glue, a gagged life where nothing tastes of nothing, but still. Who will tell me why the castles of childhood are still standing? Why my memories have the bittersweet aroma of ambiguity and why age seven, that of French toast, the slice of brioche my grandmother dipped in milk and egg yolk, then slipped into the oven, and which melted in my mouth crunching under my teeth, fragile, creamy, buttered and blackened enough on the top to leave behind a bit of bitterness on your tongue? Why the beach at Birochère stretches to the end of the world, to where it sinks all at once into an abyss lashed by a sea of flames? Why my Godless Christmases, with their plush, their felt, their paste gems and their rotten whorey frills, each year still assume as much importance as passing from the Age of Pisces into the Age of Libra? The only thing that has changed is the notion of time. At ten, endless steppes separate one year from another, months count like centuries, and you experience the eternal return of the seasons like a mystic rite of passage and ritual, an alchemical transmutation; in April my eyes were peeled for the first ray of sunlight which struck the kitchen table at four, the time for slices of Vienna bread sprinkled with a thin, velvety layer of powdered cocoa; I waited for December so that night would fall quickly, as smooth as cat's fur, cold and indulgent, so that with a little luck it would snow and I could pretend to have the flu and stay at the window and surrender myself to the first thrill children are allowed, the thrill of letting yourself be spellbound by this whirl, white, haunting, lusterless, swift and oblique, or slow and straight, which so transfigured rue Mauberge that it became unbearably beautiful, diamond-encrusting the balconies' wrought-iron volutes, thus transformed into mysterious chalices, grails of frost at the rim of which I ran my finger collecting the cold powder more blue than white that melted on my tongue with the taste of an anaesthetizing, vanilla-flavored sherbet. The Snow Queen's sleigh dashed along under the muslin lozenges, and I glued my nose to the cracked-open window hoping that, like Kay, I would be pierced by a splinter of the magic mirror dropped by the demons and shattered into smithereens upon the earth—by the mere fact of keeping my eyes wide open, I most likely wound up being pierced by a shard, but it had surely lost its satanic properties, for instead of changing the beautiful into the ugly, my mother into a manatee, Cassinoux into a cassowary and Benazouli into a boa constrictor, it transformed a waterspout into a palace, a trashcan into a carriage, the plumber into Gary Cooper (the love of my life) and a mangy dog into a Florentine prince—however, I didn't become aware of these surprising powers until much later. For the instant, the instant of my childhood, meaning an infinity of instants, a blanket of thick mist spread itself out between me and the world, an opaque monsoon cloud like the kind clinging to the sides of the Himalayas and concealing the Sikkimese Valley, from time to time dissipated by a rent of sunshine that sweeps the landscape with an episodic light.

But these rifts in the mist, Superego tells me, always ready to soften edges and use an eraser wherever necessary, you don't really think they're enough to make up for all the rest?

Remember the woman selling *La Figaro* in pirate's pants,
perched on her high heels and wearing a man's cap, who
siphoned off all the pensioners on the Promenade des
Anglais behind her rolling Hollywood hips. And on the
Champs de Mars in Nemours, on midsummer's night, your
ecstasy before the Antbear or the Anteater which aroused as
much curiosity in the villagers as in the idle gawkers when
the first giraffes arrived from Africa and were exhibited in
cages in the Forum. And the torchlight tattoo behind the
firemen, the firefly dance of the accordion lamps, the volleys
of firecrackers, and the hand of the grocer's son Lucien
feeling up your breasts while pretending to grope around in
the darkness—you scared, huh, you scared? Don't worry,
they won't stick any firecrackers under your feet as long as
I'm here. And your eyes as big as saucers before the ultimate
gift: fireworks, trails of smoke whistling, scratching the sky
real high and bursting into flowers, stars, astral anemones,
trickles of diamonds, showers of shimmering light, a fallout
of ashen flakes the color of phosphorus; meanwhile at
ground level was the sulfurous fog of the green Bengal
lights, and you, agape, unhitched from reality, exploded
into incandescent atoms, you did not budge an inch—and
he knew it too, the rascal, that you wouldn't budge. With
Lydie, he would say, no need to worry that she'll tell you to
get lost. You stick her in front of something THAT IS SEEN,
you take her to the movies or to a sound-and-light show; as
soon as she's got something to gawk at, you could stick your
finger into her little thingy without vaseline. Well, Henri, his
buddy would say, with Arlette it's pastries. She falls for
cream puffs, ditto for chocolate éclairs. Once her face is
stuffed, no doubt about it, you got it made. Jeez, Lucien said
with a sympathetic air, your old lady's a walking stomach. An
alimentary canal. A pigging-out machine. I can't see how a
guy can bang a chick with a chocolate mustache from

gobbling down Toblers all day long, it would make me puke. And plus it ends up being pretty expensive. You see, Lydie, she's visual, Kodak film is what she gobbles. The rest of the time, you're out of luck. Practically frigid, you know. The whole secret is knowing the tricks, he concluded with a hearty slap between his buddy's shoulder blades, and then finally WITH WOMEN YOU JUST NEVER KNOW, a pronouncement that always punctuated more or less aptly the end of his speeches, summing up for him the changing, moist, unsettling and vaginal universe of unpredictable Chicks.

—Yes, but you're going too far there, I say to Superego. There I'm twelve years old, pal. Almost as old as Juliet. The score I've got to settle is with my mummyish period. At twelve there's the lycée, anonymity in classes of forty pupils, Teenform bras and freedom. . . . You know, the beginning of the delinquency years.

—All you are is a sack of bile, Superego grumbles, a punctured squid pissing ink. But you'll never manage to puke it all up. And affection, you know what that is yet? You were given so much that you turned up your nose. You give the impression you almost kicked off because affection gave you a tummy ache.

—Oh yes, let's talk about that. I was given so much, I would say, that I was thrown into life, that is, into school, completely naked, plucked bare, my ribs exposed to the air, ready to be crucified on Golgotha. A carnivorous affection, yes. This damned affection made me so anemic that I broke down into tears whenever I dropped my pencil. I had neither blood nor bowels nor sex, since they were never mentioned to me. I floated through the ether like one of Fra Angelico's angels. Beams of light came out of my palms. If I had been tossed into an arena swarming with lions, they would have licked my toes instead of gobbling me up. A

saint. A Paschal Lamb. An asshole. Mommy-Daddy's delightful
little girl. I was NOT CAPABLE OF THE LEAST EMOTION,
do you understand what that means? I didn't feel that I was
living my life. I was drifting in a sort of infra-subreality, in an
intermediate world between heaven and hell, in Tibetan
bardo, in the seconds of coma preceding death. A sadistic
deity had surrounded me with a mosquito net that kept me
from feeling the simple air all around me. I was hibernating
as if stunned by a strong dose of Valium. That being said, my
parents aren't solely responsible, when I think about
Cassinoux who helped her mother give herself an abortion
and went on her own to bury the fetus in an empty lot, and
there I was baby-wabied, little-darlinged, lugged around to
Lake Annecy and Mont-Blanc, I ought to keep my mouth
shut but that's just the point, do you see Mont-Blanc, that
blue range on the horizon, those sparkling glaciers, my
mother that fine woman, enraptured by the wonders of
nature and me squinting, forcing myself to feel an emotion,
even the littlest, even the most timid genesis of an eddy,
before that brilliant ridge way over there—and always this
cotton in my head keeping me from seizing upon reality,
this impression of a permanent dream, a nightmare, a lie
sustained by a silent conspiracy. Unconsciously, I did everything in my power to resemble the image others had of me, to
stick to the prototype of the little girl with her normal likes
and games and joys; my parents had been sold a doll that
drinks, eats, walks and talks with an operator's manual, but
everything worked backwards. The only fun the little girl
had was with her Caran d'Ache makeup and her feathers,
rigging traps for the infinite in the delicate spirals of a snail's
shell, making battalions of insects rise up upon paper, batra-
chians, reptiles and the whole series of unsettling metamorphosing creatures among which she lived her parallel
existence. It was all a disconcerting misapprehension.

—Fine, Superego says. Let me project a few images your way. I slip the plates into the magic lantern and here goes. Bellow all you want, I'm tying you to your chair and you're going to watch this little retrospective file past to the very end.

Oh, the dirty dog, he snatches me up, binds me with the cunning, ambiguous ties of affection. Affection, profile hair-netted with tulle, speckled with velvet and felt-lined with my grandmother's apricot rice powder; the red cat-eared balloons in the zoological gardens, the first crocuses in the flower beds of Sacré-Coeur; the red-hot chestnuts, split open and sallow, burning your fingers through the newspaper cone, a wintertime delight on the Grands Boulevards —God, how big they were those Boulevards. Sparks of affection: the paste-gem bracelet and the butterfly of multicolored stones my grandmother presents me—my dad's mother, to whose house we go for tea every Sunday and spend Christmas Eve; the flames of blue affection on the Christmas pudding; a glow of salmon-pink affection under the fluted silk shades and the 1925 lamp circled by a black ring like the planet Saturn.

Childhood trips. A strange, elusive land where everything is eaten, caressed, fondled, and sniffed. A ghost train charging into the darkness, sometimes colliding with unforeseen obstacles—skeletons, witches, fairies, ectoplasms —which appear for the brief span of a visual deflagration only to sink back into the gloom where the spirits of memory scratch you, tickle you, electrocute you, rub up against you at times with their spider legs, at others with their dying-man's fingers. Tunnel of Love washed by the river Time, slowly flowing like the Loire, which we are taught in school sluggishly circles around sandbanks and laps under the arches of the châteaux made of stone and slate, Chenonceaux with its name of precious marquetry,

Amboise creamy and caressing like amber and boysenberry, Azay tapering like the blade of a short dagger in a white velvet scabbard, Chambord snowy and royal like sable, marten and Dutch linen.

The holidays of childhood are the only canal locks of Time, which set to simmering as they concentrate behind them as much energy as the Iguacú Falls as soon as the sluices are closed. Christmas, birthdays, Easter, vacations and even, and especially, illnesses, chicken pox, measles, mumps, feverous weak spells ridden with ear infections— Dad has just bought me *Captain Fracasse* in the Gerfaut collection and *Wolfhound Bari* by Curwood in the Red and Gold series. I also read *General Dourakine* in the paper-bound books of the Pink Library (two francs twenty-five a volume, red percaline binding, and gilt edges cost one franc twenty-five extra) whose Gustave Doré style illustrations I knew by heart, images which were gray, crosshatched and vermiculated as if engraved with a burin or etched in needlepoint, picturing Madame Papovski wedged in a trap-door having her hindquarters lashed with a whip while "heaving horrible screams," her maddened thyroid pointing out like Benazouli's, and farther on the very same Papovski giving her driver a good belt ("she administered two vigorous slaps to the poor fellow's red sweaty cheeks").

Sick or not, I was living in a world off the beaten track where flowers, animals, and objects had received the gift of speech and never lost an opportunity to use it—the logorrhea of the pots, the dialectical discourses of the alarm clock, the litanies of the bolster pillows, the prose poems of Jules the chamber pot, a genuine cacophony. But when I was in a fever, that's when I became out-and-out hyper-perceptive. Mornings, ten-horned stags in velvet pourpoint played on a flute to awaken me, and my old pal the witch Baba Yaga, who lived in an isba resting upon chicken feet

made to look like piles, came to bring me my coffee, after
which I would tear off around Montholon Square with a
pack of forty gray wolves; at noon I would have an audience
with the Tzar Thundering Ogon, who received me with
great pomp and circumstance; I lunched upon Danon
ortolans with rose jelly and ladyfingers with the Tzarina
Molyna of the Lightning; then I would leave on an expedition into the Silkebourg Forest; that's where sometimes all
hell would break loose between me and the ogre who had a
thing for children's feet in aspic and managed sometimes to
nab me to cut mine off right above the ankle—fortunately
the Carthusian Cat, the one snoring curled up on my bed,
would always arrive in time to stick them back on me, and
when there was no cat around, Carabas would lend me his.
Evenings I would go dancing at the court of King Pest who
watched me with lascivious eyes; seated on his barrel, he
could always present me with his kingdom of red death, but
the dirty old bastard never will he succeed in kissing me—
on my hand is what I mean—and just to show off I would
discreetly stuff my sleeves with gnawed chicken bones
which, as soon as I shook them, flew up in the shape of black
swans before a dumbstruck audience.

As soon as the thermometer reached 102°, I would wait
expectantly for the witches to arrive. I had three in my life.
Baba Yaga of the Blizzard came from the shores of the
Caspian Sea and stunk of sturgeon, such a powerful odor
that I had to burn incense paper after she passed through,
and not before she kicked up her heels of course because it
would have been a grave offense to have her understand that
she reeked of fish. While Baba Yaga only knew the world of
cold, an ice cap stretching, as far as I knew, from Roubaix to
the Arctic Circle, Genghivane represented all of Asia. I
would meet that one a little later, in the flesh, in the guise of
a Sikkimese princess with an amputated hand, in the shape

of a Chinese woman, Taoist painter and musician, a
specialist in the Tibetan horn. The third, Marilia the
Brazilian, daughter of the demon Echou and reincarnation
of a mulatto prostitute, a figure I would come across again
some ten years later, around Salvador de Bahia, usually
collapsed on my bed dead-drunk, after knocking off a quart
of batida, a mixture of pure eau-de-vie and coconut milk.

Sometimes I cheated, I stuck the thermometer between
the radiator flutes. But there's no lying to witches. At 102°
Baba Yaga arrived in her isba hobbling on its piles, one
chicken foot after the other, and opened the door to leap
onto my bed; Genghivane drew closer with small mincing
steps because of her bound feet, jingling her Buddhist bells,
shaking her tambourine and beating her gong—no,
Genghivane, not the horn please, I have a splitting head-
ache, that horn sounds like the mooing of a herd of cosmic
cows—as you wish, you don't know what beauty is, she
would say, putting her tiny hands into her red brocart
sleeves to signal her disapproval while nodding her head,
which made sway the silk pendants ornamenting the tips of
her hair rolled into curls. HAHAHAHA, that was the
Gargantuan laugh of Marilia the Whore who, not a second
on my blanket, her toucan on her shoulder, would snort and
grumble: it stinks of brine here. You're the one stinking of
smallpox, Baba Yaga would cut in. Then a fistfight would
ensue, mephitic traces of which would often remain, like a
molar, a bloody earring or a tuft of hair on my pillow, after
which Marilia would end up by burning a small cone of
"defumador" which smelled something awful of hashish,
and Genghivane, even though she had perfumed her seven
orifices so she wouldn't smell anything but herself, lit a stick
of incense at the foot of the stuffed tiger head she was never
separated from and which she set very prominently on the
dresser. Then the feast would begin. A genuine witches'

Woodstock, because sometimes they would bring friends along. Baba Yaga quavered her never-ending stories while breathing out a cold mist and loosening her caviar-scented body stocking; Genghivane banged on her gong from which she never managed to obtain the primordial sound; Marilia in the middle of an epileptic fit told me porno tales and, provided I pour her a drop of table wine since in our country, barbarians that we were, we didn't know what batida was, sometimes she would agree to release around my bed a whole bag of butterflies from the Amazon, much to the toucan's furor, hating as it did these large felty flowers loathsomely brushing past. Marilia was by far the most demanding, but also the most effective. When I would ask a favor of her—for example, that it rain Sunday so that we wouldn't go eat at my aunt's and my parents would take me to the movies; that Benazouli, victim of a new quirk of her hyperactive thyroid, would be laid up the day of the math final; and that slut Zabrovsky would break her face on my bar of soap or stay stuck in a toilet stall a whole day long— Marilia would demand, for her macumba, wagonloads of sundry objects which she carefully listed, under the pretext that if Echou didn't receive two dozen Baccarat roses, roast chicken (thighs), two bottles of scotch, one of champagne and one of brandy, he would be dead set against entering into her—and I would be wondering through which end, I saw him tumbling into Marilia's innards like Santa Claus down a chimney, and when she would tell me, "By the one where you make children, you know," that didn't shed any light on things, but I was a little scared to ask her to be more specific; she really scared me stiff, that Marilia did, especially when she started rocking back and forth and cackling and slapping her thighs, the characteristic symptoms of going into a trance, during the course of which she slipped a hand under her skirts to fiddle with something, a tinkering which gave the impression of helping her since afterward she started to drool, foam at the mouth, and see the future as clearly as the bottom of a glass of water.

Once settled in, my trollops told me about the world I still didn't have access to yet, like Ondine who, imprisoned in her coral gardens, heard nothing of the universe but a muffled echo. Genghivane spoke to me about the Far East, exciting words that had to be earned by sacrificing to all the Asiatic precedences, which lasted a good fifteen minutes— z'ai zhuozi xiexe, jiuyang-jiuyang ninhaoa?—take a chair— for God's sake, where did she see a chair?—thank you, delighted to see you, how are you, etc. You'll see, she would say, the beaches of northern Java where your feet sink down into sand as white as burning snow and the swift flagella of the sunfish in the green waves of the China Sea, you will climb into the Buddha's ear to pick off from his earlobe Ceylonese rubies in bunches—considering the weight, that lobe of his must have been as soft as chewing gum—at that point Fatima, the nomad, would arrive. Qasgai, eyes darkened with kohl, who would speak to me of the cruel wonders of Islam. My poor Lydie, she would say, all this vapid Oriental nonsense is a load of garbage compared to the spells of Arabia and the deserts of Iran where thousands upon thousands of Zoroaster's useless, magical, flittering sparks are ablaze. On foot you will travel across expanses of sand, bitumen and oil, you will speak to the enamel griffins guarding the doors of the ziggurat at Tchoga-Zanbil, you will mount upon the Peacock Throne in the palace of Golestan, followed by nebulous panthers which will lick your heels, and you will set your feet upon a cushion of turquoise-colored lizards . . .

—The Orishas of Brazil will welcome you warmly, you will dance with Santa Barbara, the goddess of smallpox who spins like a dervish until she collapses from exhaustion, and you will rejoin your mother Iemanja in Salvador de Bahia, Marilia grumbled in her voice as harsh and sweet as batida. You'll see how warm the nights are around Caba Frio, when you rock in a hammock while listening to . . .

—The bullfrogs, Genghivane would hiss. Untouchables' doodoo, that's your Brazil. A civilization not even two hundred years old. No, what she'll catch is the bamboo virus. Asia is what she'll like, the Himalayas, rice paddies, the monsoon, Malaysia, king crabs with a stinger as long as a pike . . .

—And swamps and amoebae and malaria, Baba Yaga would break in. Speak to me of the Russian nights. Of crystal. Of spun glass. Of . . .

—Shut your trap, you old brine, you cod oil, Marilia bellowed, this kid's world is the Tropics—Tropics mean passion, danger, excess, the Tropics, that mythical line that cuts the world in two like an orange, the Tropics where the leaves on the banana trees are as wide as laundry paddles, where giant chiseled palms bend their trunks springing from the earth like chlorophyll geysers, the Tropics where there's a smell of burning, where the heavy air envelops you like a flaccid caress and where night capsizes in the Bay of Rio, spilling cartloads of beryl, calcites, and amethysts.

—Honorable, rotten mussel, Genghivane softly replied while chewing her wad of betel, the aigrettes of her tall headdress trembling with anger, all those trashy pebbles are rat turds compared to ivory, pale ivory, and polished, ivory the color of yak butter, and sacred jade, the unctuous, the hard and the resonant, and your whole cardboard jungle would never be worth one of the screw pines from Borneo —and art, what do you know about art in Brazil? Have you ever seen anything like the frescoes of our Tibetan monasteries, those warped paintings writhing on the walls like glowworms? And most important of all, the art of living, it surely wasn't your African ancestors that brought you even a veneer—those primates. As for your gaucho cooking, let's talk about that. She will eat at the table of kings, the dear child, she will taste swallows' nests, sweet and sour fish, fried gizzards, tortoise soup, sharks' fins in cinnamon-tree blossoms, candied pig's bladder . . .

—Pig's bladder yourself, Marilia yelped, and marmoset brain, lacquered bat, stuffed water-buffalo balls, among other delicacies. A healthy diet. With your anemic tendencies, it's rare grilled churrasco meat that the kid needs to give her heart strength. . . . And then you Sons of Heaven, the whole lot of you, you're nothing but stomachs. Eating, eating, that's fine, but what about fucking? That did it, look at her turning more yellow than usual.

—Stupid numbskulls, Baba Yaga hissed, caviar by the ladle is what she'll savor, and white caviar at that, the kind from the Imperial Court of Iran!

—RAW MEAT! Marilia bellowed, letting the blood dribble down her chin.

—PIG BLADDER! Genghivane squealed while beating her gong.

Unfortunately, the fever would begin to let up and the witches to lower their voices a tone; Baba Yaga would leave for the Caspian shores at the modest pace her chicken feet permitted; Genghivane went back to her Buddha's ear, Marilia and her toucan to the Bahia bordello where Echou was waiting for her, her mystic spouse, the great screw artist of the Orishas. But I continued on all alone, I walked through landscapes so beautiful that they were questions without answers, I passed along metaphysical shores pockmarked with motionless atoms, enveloped in a silence wherein matter was dissolving, and dead beaches where the waves lashed the shells of foundered boats with the sound of arrows rattling in the quiver of a god, with my fingers I

stroked the Tuscan hills, I wandered in the courtyards of
Florentine palaces, an abstract, dislocated space where,
upon geometrical flagstones, young people in red body
stockings slipped through regular porticos, architectural
constructs with no thickness fixed against a pure sky, while
above crumbling brick crenels the clouds of immateriality
drifted by; I walked barefooted in the silver filings of the
eternal snows, I wore out my soles in the bazaars of the
Orient, amidst nomads in gauze petticoats dotted with
velvet, I penetrated into the Chinese tombs where princesses slept under their jade armor, I hovered above Angkor
in the form of a kite with owl eyes, I followed the covered
way of Elsenor castle lending my arm to the ghost completely crippled with rheumatism ever since the time he
spent his winters in contemplation of the frozen sea, I
rested in the Persian caravansary whose hillocks were
worn down by the sand-filled wind, I slept beneath the stars
under the thin frosty layer of Scandinavian nights, in the
burning pitch of Oriental nights, upon the cold marble of
Sikh temples or in mosques whose walls, covered with a
thousand multifaceted mirrors, sparkled like the bottom of
a salt mine—but the vaulting ribs of glazed earthenware
Muslim cupolas vanished in a mist beneath their network of
Koranic flowers in the pale light of morning, apple sauce
replaced hallucinogens, the dumb odor of Balsamorhinol,
the smell of sturgeon, defumador and incense, and the
luster of the Tropical belt diminished until it was as muted
as the white dwarves that take ages on end to be consumed
with the implacable death of the stars.

*

At this stage of convalescence, I would emigrate to the Sarcophagus, a low divan covered with a fake threadbare panther skin, so named because, cramped as it was, it just barely allowed a twelve-year-old mummy to lie stretched out, and there was a vaguely Egyptian shape to its back. So I was convalescing, my back resting in the hollow of the Sarco and my feet upon the Salamander, a wood stove an aunt from Blancmesnil had bequeathed us and which had been used for heat during the war, a noble cast-iron utensil decorated with a lizard spitting fire, and I would listen to Sarco speak to me from time to time where, on his antique panther, presently reduced to the state of a pelt, the fannies of illustrious models for pompous artists in the Gerard mode had set themselves down, and even Sarah Bernhardt's mythical rear, but that's where I think he was sort of spinning tales. As for the Salamander, she would tell the same stories as my grandmother about the Occupation, ration cards, chickens sent by country relatives, the exodus in trucks, blackouts, memories that didn't interest me all that much, all the less so because on account of hearing all this talk about how much trouble it was getting something to eat during the war my picture of a heroic and resisting France gradually crumbled away, replaced by an image of a Petainist country, cowardly, collaborationist, and fiercely preoccupied with its stomach cramps. So while the Salamander wheezed and spluttered her rattling mono-logue, I would take a snooze, which threw her into a wild rage, but all I asked of her was to warm my tootsies and the more hopping mad she got, the better she kept things cooking.

*

Having an adventure was taking the bus with my mother to go to the Bois de Vincennes; come rain or wind, I preferred the rear platform: at least back there you could breathe and you could watch the conductor pull his cord at each stop like on a flush toilet, you would always be waiting for a soft hiss to come from somewhere or for a fizzing explosion like bottles of Pschitt Orange or Pschitt Lemon whose posters plastered the city walls beside the Cinzano zebra.

I loathed well-groomed French gardens, so the Buttes-Chaumont especially turned me on because of their romantic jumble, as charming as a drawing by Hubert Robert, offering capricious pathways climbing in hump-backs or dropping toward narrow lanes fissured with diamondlike creeks spanned by fragile bridges that had to be crossed with caution, as if walking on a rainbow.

I didn't like the Champ-de-Mars as much, where I would ride the amusements and the rocking horse with my cousins; it was flat, bare, predictable and always swept by a wind that would "take the horns right off of a bull," as my Aunt Ro would say while holding down her hat and narrowing her eyes as if somewhere out in the tundra you could make out a herd of grazing mammals—I for one would have loved to see some bison, but zilch, not one single horned creature, from which I concluded that Aunt Ro was a liar.

I knew Montholon Square by heart. Since then its belly has been knocked in and its trees killed to make a parking lot; all that's left of the square of my childhood is the statue of the Catherinettes, the old maids, with their poise and their fake ass, and the lawn has grown back, but they forgot to replant the privets whose lemony scent gladdened my grandmother's olfactory senses in the spring.

During privet time, the head monitor Madame Pichenouffe brought my entire class there, twice a week, in the morning. The Pichenouffe lady looked like a joke on Louis XI, and had a wen on her forehead that would have made her seem like a rhinoceros if her scarlet coloring had not betrayed her undeniable kinship with Satan. So we would flock under the crook of this unicorned devil as far as Montholon Square, hoping that one day she would lose a shoe and we would at last find out if instead of feet she had cloven hooves, a mystery that was to remain unbroken, as was certainly the virginity of blessed Pichenouffe.

The bench to the left of the statue of the Catherinettes was taken up every morning by five small old men in berets discussing horse racing and meteorology. The youngest wore black glasses, a beige suit and a red fuchsia tie, which made him sort of look like an over-the-hill pimp, but for us he was the Hypnotist, a spy from the East whose plans absolutely had to be uncovered to safeguard the country. So we crept under the bench, scraping our knees and ripping our panties, which set off our mothers' ululations of horror, who with a surgical gesture welded Band-Aids as sticky and skin-tight as putty to our knees haloed in pale vermilion by mercurochrome, all the while promising to dress us up like pit-face miners the days we went to the square.

To the right of the square, the billboard column concealed the fruit of the side activities of the gang, a traffic in furs. By pressing our noses against the vent, we could make out a whole pile, all in a jumble: white bear, wolf, beaver, zebra, monkey, mink—inaccessible treasures since we did not know the code, the open-sesame of the column, and we knew there was no point in speaking about it to adults who continued to stream past these stashed-away secrets without suspecting their existence. One time Cassinoux told me how she had found rubies inside a sidewalk urinal, a pretext to bet me three caramel bars that I wouldn't dare set foot there, a foot all right, but sticking my nose in seemed to me a lot harder, so I forked over the candy.

Childhood is a vast treasure hunt. What was precious for me and Cassinoux was everything that could be caressed, that delighted the eye, the nose, the taste buds or the ear. We set off to discover the world, groping forward, rapacious, avid, often disappointed, walking blindfolded through a forest of symbols, accosted or allured by a sound, a smell, a voice, a fragrance that spoke of elsewhere; even I, specialist as I was at skidding over reality, I got hooked now and then by a sensation more violent than another, which stirred very distant echoes in my subconscious after having crossed through successive layers of coma. Then I would look, feel, sniff, touch my treasures hidden in a scallop shell box Cassinoux had at her disposal. Both of us got excited over thin silver chocolate wrappers that we could delicately crumple into metallic embossments, over aventurines, small rock caramels shimmering with coppery flecks, we got excited over glass balls that made it snow on the Eiffel Tower when you shook them, which gave us the impression of penetrating the mysteries of a transparent and thus clearly defined and comprehensible cosmos; what a kick we got from this microclimate that we ourselves could control, and while all around the world's appearances remained static, the snow flakes turned in their topsy-turvy waltz inside the ball where, for the space of a minute, the headspinning rush of unreality was concentrated. We had a particular affection for the smooth bluish ivory of certain beans, those shaped like the moon or Jesus in embryo, and we remained fascinated by the whirl of fixed flowers that die inside sulfurs as if struck by lightning into immortality.

In Nemours my grandfather had bought a plot of land along the Loing. Every morning he straddled his bike, his fishing rod fastened to the frame, his box of maggots on the baggage rack, with the solemn announcement that he was off to "view the grounds," as if the dahlias, radishes, and the tall red spears of his cana brava needed the master's daily glance to grow.

On one side, the grounds sloped gently downward toward the Loing, before which grandfather would install himself on his folding chair to track down the perch and roach fish which a little later were to be sizzling in the frying pan of my grandmother who would be besieged by a bacchanalian bevy of cats clawing her stretch-nylon stockings and clinging to her apron. With the purchase of these few hectares, my grandfather had most likely assuaged a repressed instinct to be a landowner and satisfied his old dream of later seeing the construction, beside HIS fisherman's hut and HIS lettuce patch, of the house he dreamed about, with backside nestled on HIS bench, the famous bench that would remain the one and only symbol of the place where his superb mythical abode was supposed to have been built, a dream that vanished into stars of imponderable feathers, into elusive crystals of dust, the way dandelion balls do when you puff on their stems.

Later on, Grandpop stopped riding his bike. He made do with trudging from the bedroom to the kitchen at mealtimes, taking up the whole of the hallway; I see him again, like Goliath, so brawny in my memory as a kid, that I was always expecting him to recover his strength of yesteryear, to push apart the walls of that damned hallway too cramped for his body, as the second half of his life had been, in fact, after the war.

For before ending his days wedged in a hallway, my grandfather had loved war. Testifying to this was the Legion of Honor, fistfuls of medals, decorations and citations, kept between piles of sheets in my grandmother's closet. Grandpop, with those blue Chinese porcelain eyes, gray-blonde mustache smelling of tobacco, vest very tight across his belly, and pocketwatch, had really started to live once he had found himself face-to-face with death. The quality of his life, as we say today, was something he never gave much thought to. On the other hand, the quality of his death, that was something he knew about. He really would have deserved to come to an end in the field of honor—boom! a bomb on his skull, or a bullet in his flesh at Verdun when he barreled like a cannon shell from the bottom of his trench, drawing all his pals along with him, kids shivering with fear and cold who had gone off to war whistling tunes without thinking. But no, the bitch death was waiting to catch up with him much farther on and much more meanly; instead of an exploding bouquet falling in a smut of blood and glory, she wanted to make my grandfather into a bedridden hemiplegic for their pathetic wedding, oh how handsome the groom was with a catheter in his stomach, a tube in his throat from which a serpentine hiss arose, with his blue-white eyes dilated upon some indescribable, otherworldly vision; when I saw him in the Broussais hospital room, maybe he was already in the midst of passing through the successive stages of khorva, this firebrand become the victim of a ridiculous little vein that popped in his brain—a good thing you don't know the last paragraph of the contract ahead of time.

At any rate, the day I was brought to see my dying grandfather, in the Broussais ward, they were expecting the bride dressed in black, and all the patients sitting up or lying in their beds turned their heads toward the door, sure that it was she, with calm weary eyes, almost disappointed to see entering in her stead a procession of human beings. I did not dare look to the side; on the bed boards there was scratching, and oozing, and purulenting, and an odor of European death, a foul death, the kind with green flies and white worms that gets into your throat with a taste of cold earth; my grandfather's eyes stuck out from his head like marbles and the tube in his mouth like a periscope; the sunshine was in on the party, and a big puddle of pus ran over me and was about to drip all the way down to my socks if I didn't get away from there real fast; they were lying to me yet one more time, they were inventing old age and anguish for me, there should have been another way to come to an end—but I would still have to wait ten years before seeing the Nepalese in flames by the shores of the Bagmati, fire and red fever by the sacred stream, a bit of ash thrown into the mountain water, and an old man scrawny as a rake walking on the Agra road and collapsing in slow motion in the dust because he had quite simply come to the end of his journey, and his breath was already leaving the filigree envelope of the lungs to rejoin the monsoon clouds on the point of bursting in one clap like the thunder of God.

*

Grandfather was buried in Caudebec-en-Caux, where I went to pick out the tombstone with my grandmother. She hesitated for a long time, discussing price and color, only to finally settle on the one I preferred, a marble rectangle whose luster and quartz inlay made it resemble a magnificent slice of pâté in aspic. All metaphysical questions stopped there, useless, before this pâté whose length and breadth and price we knew, in the small cemetery in Normandy.

All that's left me of Grandpop is a book with a dedication, the *Iliad* and the *Odyssey* in the Pléiade edition, and the painless memory of an odor of tobacco—later on I was told he loved me and, as far as pigheadedness went, I was a chip off the old block; consequently I developed a sort of posthumous tenderness for him, glaringly pointless since he was not there to take note of its expression. But Grandpop, a professional amateur, oddball and dilettante, a dastardly loafing adventurer, remained standing like the castle of Gilles de Rais in Pornic, dungeon of childhood, a stuffed ancestor representing the already vanished race of men from the beginning of the century, sporting mustaches, stocky, virile, hearty drinkers of Ricard, belote players, devotees of the National Lottery and the Tierce, misogynists and maid chasers but attached to their wives, called "dutiful," but what duties might they have had, the poor creatures, other than to have their wits about them when they became managers of cafés or war widows with children? So Grandfather venerated Work, Family, and Country, in fact work (hmmm), family (hmmm), country (oh sure), was it really for his country that he risked his neck at Verdun (certainly not), considering that his medals no sooner pinned on were stripped off pronto for insubordination and that he was sent to stew in the stockade while awaiting the opportunity for a new exploit.

But that wild adventurer, that ersatz legionnaire who would bellow HANG UP at my grandmother loud enough for it to resound at the other end of the line when her lady friends kept her on the phone—I was utterly convinced this bandit full of an evangelical innocence must be getting some fishing in at the springs of Paradise despite his raging outbursts, his passion for Beaujolais and the few little bastards he turned out around the world—if children and irresponsible people with Good Intentions are still accepted there.

End of summer in the Vendée. The time of mauve asters, equinoctial tides, blackberries that taste like dust and whose sugary velvet squishes between your fingers and leaves seeds between your teeth. I strolled around with Vincent, the successor of Lulu from Nemours, a doctor's son from Aubusson who rented the semi-detached Ker Yves house every year. Vincent, sixty-six pounds of feverish nerves and dreams, who was inflicted, for reasons of health, with a daily barrage of baths in a glacial iodized sea that changed the direction your blood was circulating simply by dipping your toe in, which he emerged from half-dead, shivering and already blue with cold only to dive head first into a terry-cloth sack with a drawstring that his mother held out to him with a toreador's sweeping gesture. But he survived. A person really had to be sturdy to withstand vacation, the so-called Swedish movements, the ice baths, and the Club Mickey games—sack races, obstacle course, crawling exercises under a trellis set a couple of inches above the sand; but fortunately, side by side, we were able to cope, to cut the classes of Monsieur Colas, whose mustache and pectorals tightly molded by his red undershirt lay waste to our mothers' hearts.

But Vincent and I escaped from our holidays because at twelve nothing is better than freedom. So, in the middle of

our cavalcades along the corniche, we would halt our
Arabian horses an instant, galling their mouths mercilessly
with the bit so we could lean over the emptiness and give
ourselves a good dose of vertigo and count the jellyfish,
those large white hats of repulsive gelatin abristle with
arrows of sunlight and sluggishly rocked by the waves of the
equinox. Sometimes, with our Bactrian camels, we left on
an expedition to the country priests' place, to the abbey
where a path also named Country-Priests led us, a narrow
passageway of greenery bathed in a liquor of light distilled
under the oak leaves spread apart on the quiet by Morgana's
or Melusina's stringy fingers and sometimes pierced by
Arthur's sword agleam in a sun's ray but disappearing as
soon as we drew our hands near because probably we
weren't old enough yet to be heroes. But strands of fairies'
hair clung behind on the Virginia creeper and honeysuckle
for us to gather; rips in the thin layer of duckweed covering
the pond revealed a bottom as green as anisette from where
only the Slime King's daughter could rise, changed into a
toad, and in the country priests' vegetable garden the string
beans reached to the sky all at once like the shamans' rope as
soon as we would utter the magic formula. They're growing
giant mandrakes too, Vincent told me, and the roots are sort
of like a pecker, that's why witches use them to make juice.
The only thing is that mandrakes are stashed out of sight. So
while pretending to take a little turn in the vegetable garden
to admire the flowers, we vainly sought an enormous
carriage mounted on a pecker from which juice ran, and we
left with cabbages, carrots, peas and cheese from which
straight off Vincent cut with his penknife thick creamy
slices pungently reeking of nanny goat.

On the well we tracked green lizards that edged in under
the boards we tried to spread apart to steal a glimpse of
infinity and to make out something in the uterine depths of

the world. Instead of that, when our eyes had grown used to the darkness, the only thing we made out was a distant warped reflection of ourselves in the gloomy circle of water, as if some wise-guy devil had held out a mirror to block our way on the path of truth. So, disappointed, we moved on to another kind of distraction, hoisting ourselves on the wall to get the full benefit of one of those daily thundering screaming matches that the Chambon lady put her daughters through; good old Madame Chambon slept with the gym teacher Monsieur Colas, a release undoubtedly inadequate for a vitality whose excesses she purged by chasing after her kids with swings of her broom accompanied by a repertoire of insults that must have howled in the ears of the country priests, snapping the horns right off of their notion of the sacred.

*

—Now don't you worry about it, honey, my mother would say in a voice from beyond the grave when speaking of school starting up again in September. Going to lycée isn't as bad as all that, and she would rest her eyes on me with such a look of anguish that I felt a cold sweat of terror trickle down my back. There you go again giving her the creeps about school starting, my father would cut in, while setting out his shrimp nets to dry. There'll be plenty of time to talk about it on September 15th, don't spoil the last week of vacation she has left. Hey, tomorrow we ought to go to Gourmalon for a picnic, he threw in to change the direction of the conversation.

While listening to them, my thoughts dwelled on the directress of my small private academy who refused to let me out of the house without an umbrella as soon as a drop of rain fell. Such a delicate little girrrrl, she would quaver in that tone of hers perfumed with fried garlic, she's going to be taken ill in that rain, this blue annngel. . . . I, taken ill, who dreamed only of tornadoes, earthquakes and typhoons— but just go try to make somebody believe that about a fifty-five-pound myopic snotnose with a limp, dazed eyes and fingernails speckled with anemia marks. So I was waiting for classes to start up with a mixture of fear and jubilation, hoping that, lost in the crowd of kids and no longer inevitably an Only Daughter First in the Class, I would be left alone to follow my merry old way, even if it wasn't the one that had been traced out for me.

*

The images of childhood projected by the magic lantern (or phenakistoscope), paled like the colors of summer: the swelling Seine climbing the calves of the Zouave on the Pont d'Alma while Mom twists my hair in round gray rubber curlers whose traces it would hold a long while afterward, despite the brushing that would tame them into long springy sausages; my grandmother preparing *papoutes,* semolina with milk and vanilla-flavored sugar, spreading ladyfingers with jam to stick them together two-by-two and make them into trifles with cream, turning out from their alum paper Plums-Puvier glazed with rum. The taste of childhood. Sweet sweetness. A sea of caramel, of syrup, of marmalade, a river of molasses, firns of barley water, a Titicaca of malted chocolate, quicksands of jam, oceans of sweetness that winter would freeze into nougat or sugar candy.

When you emerge from this sticky slime to drag yourself along the shore still all gluey from this coating of placental sugar, you begin by washing yourself, even if it means flaying yourself alive just so it comes off and you get a frenetic yen for everything that sets your teeth on edge, is harsh on your palate, burns your throat as it goes down, withstands the pressure of your bite, a need to yank, to tear apart, to gnaw and gobble down raw meat, if not human flesh, while making the feast flow with vinegar, pure alcohol or lemon juice spiked with firewater; that's the sign that you've put an end to the soft, the cooked, and the sweet—childhood.

*

Flashback to the wings of a theater rented for the occasion, namely the premiere of *Around the World in 80 Days* revised by Jean Nohain, acted by the troupe from the S— Academy on the day prizes were awarded. Let's not mention the squawking that surrounds this kind of display, the gawking fish faces of parents feverishly awaiting the moment to applaud their offspring in the role of Passepartout or the Bengal tiger; we were in a real theater at any rate, we were going to act out a comedy in it; there was rice powder, masks, the smell of girls' sweat, of mothers in flowery, expensive perfumes, the acid taste of Bourgeois lipstick on my mouth and a stupendous fright twisting my guts. In two minutes I was going to recite my tirade of Philéas Fogg; Philéas, that's me, in top hat and tails, my cheeks painted crimson with creamy rouge beginning to turn color. You're on, the dresser whispered to me with a push toward the stage. The curtain parted. Below, a silent, gaping black hole, animated by a slight swell of breath, something like an invisible ocean lapping in the night, from which I was separated by the row of footlights. And I began to recite my text without even realizing it, utterly in a trance, zapped by the dazzling explosion of grace; I didn't give a damn about Philéas' monologue; what mattered was this happiness of being alive, this divine impression of sticking true to reality, which had never even suggested itself before in my world of fear and cold and shadow shows. The bare truth, that was me on that stage, and below the pack of larva, with me an entity whose contours stood out precisely, who had as much right as others to exist without being judged or being accountable to anyone; in dreams the nibbling mouse, I had come out of my hole in the light of artificial suns—in short, I shouted, I laughed, I strutted, I hopped, all the while declaiming the suave-sounding crap of Philéas' monologue adapted for classroom use; I was hollering that I had a right to live, instead of running belly to the ground to escape being judged; I had made a sudden about-face and I was looking at Others there below in the gloom of the infernal abysses, Others, horrible creatures, sadists, grown-ups, the universal Supreme Court, presided over by Anubis the jackal god who passed judgment for one purpose: to punish.

At the same time that a spasm of joy fibrillated my heart, another sensation got mixed in, a wave rising from the depths of my unconscious like the inexplicable tide that every year rolled dead calves toward Caudebac, the mind-boggling memory of a moment when, tumbling from the storm-whipped top of the Aravis Pass while the bolts flew every which way and the grass flattened under the wind, I was a gob of spit, a splutter of God's saliva; I hovered with the black clouds, I rumbled with the thunder, I blazed in the intensity of the present like a lightning-struck tree, I rent the sky with blinding electrical cracks, I got smashed on the tempest as on wine or sobs, I was driven like a magic nail

into the center of the world where typhoons take shape as
well as everything else that violates, pierces, bursts and
pulverizes; the rain melted on my tongue like the black host
of a satanic anti-christening whose taste my saliva would
keep until the day I overwhelmed myself with a head-
spinning solitude, shut up by the projectors in a sealed
space, magnified, mystical, inaccessible to mortals who had
scarcely the right to murmur, relegated to the vestibule of
the Mysteries.

The curtain closed, my lipstick was wiped off, and I traded
in my shimmering dress coat for one of gray ratine—I had
gone back under my cockroach shell, but an indescribable
glow lit the horizon, an indescribable quiver of springtime
in the air announced the dawn of future metamorphoses.

The Laceration

December 1974. Vienna. Suicide capital. Faded velvets and cracked crystals of old Europe. In the salon of the Sacher Hotel, the memory of things past condenses between walls covered with photos inscribed with royal signatures. In the Sacher salon, the vestibule of the centuries that pile up one on top of the other on coatracks like musicians' capes whose hems have dragged along in the mud; Europe, grandmother of sluts, warms her feet before a fireguard while fattening her face with Sachertorte, that chocolate Christian stuffer, because like children and the elderly she favors the kind of cake where she runs no risk of leaving her dentures behind. She has lived a thousand years and comes on like a fifteen-year-old. Her makeup has just about all peeled off and her lipstick flaked from her lips, and yet she still delights, the charming creature, the chatterbox, the waltz whirler, even if her music is nothing more than parody, the shrill scratches of out-of-tune violins of the orchestra de la Municipalità e di Poveri drowning out the last strains of *The Magic Flute,* even if the fake beams of her artificial baroque suns no longer warm even the ballet tricked up with wax virgins nor the fingers of the angels in drag, their cheeks powdered purple, frozen in a stopped flight of golden chiffons and metallic blues, even if her musicians have fallen into the orchestra pit upon a pile of plague-ridden cadavers and the echo of her waltzes only sets to dancing the ghosts of the Black Death—in spite of all of that, I melt with tenderness for you, old Europe, your entire paraphernalia of writhing sparks and your icy fevers, I quake with pity and respect before your rococo decay and your consumptive neurasthenia; I will still hold you between my fingers like an ember of moribund sensuality until the last glow dies out, for your life shows how little life is worth, like the death's-head crowned with laurel, deep in the crypts where kings sleep, keeping watch over tombs of bronze and brass, great machines relegated to the wings of a forgotten theater, I love you because you are the very expression of hollowness, like waterspouts spiraling into the void, and I love the lie of her preserved Christmases, the Germanic Christmases, their large pines hung with balls frosted with silver and sparkling paste gems, and the snow promised for and falling due on December 25th, where I dig my boot heels in Belvédère Park—I also am five, twenty and a thousand years old, I have just been born and I have undergone every metamorphosis, my lives come only at the beginning and the end of worlds, in a brutal primitive age or in a rocaille degeneracy, I gather only buds and faded blossoms, I look only at the sun at dawn or at dusk, I know only what is burlesque, what is tender or tragic, the privileged moments when life is just what it ought to be: movement, mutation, germination, beginning, stuttering, bursting forth, decomposition, and death. Mediterranean light, classical Greece, adulthood, the golden mean, and balance bore me; all I want is the ambiguity of passing stages, stage tricks, tricks with mirrors, the acuteness and the non-existence of the present—so where else better than here? Europe, that old heart patient, is holding up under the injections of camphorated alcohol and there I am on this stage of rotted planks to tell about the raw, the alive, the scarlet, the scalding, the laceration—adolescence.

In Belvédère Park, the girls Lydie and Polline chase after the crows that scatter in a limp, obscene flight and settle squawking upon the heads of the female sphinxes. Polline, twelve years old, sitting on the palace steps with her legs spread—just tough if the guard sees her panty bottom— sticks her fingers in her nose while scratching herself with the single-minded energy of a gibbon, then springs off hopping on one leg under the plane trees of the lycée court-yard while pushing her marker across the worn hopscotch drawing of the West. From the direction of the dining hall, a smell of fried whiting fills the air.

September 15, 1962, I entered society through the door to room 34 of the lycée Lamartine. Surprise. It was quite a change from the gloomy minuscule classrooms of the S— Academy permeated by the harsh, suffocating odor of chalk whose particles offended your nostrils like a whiff of camphor, where the desks were made of sprung wood with a hole for an inkwell, a porcelain chalice with a glossy rim at the bottom of which stagnated the heavy purplish pool of the Waterman called china blue—today I settled my buns on a chair with iron legs resting on linoleum, and my elbows on a flat table of a light-colored wood, carved out with a shallow groove for fountain pens. But what was most astounding was the questionnaire to be filled out. Last name, first name, address, telephone, grade school attended, intended profession. It really killed me. Apparently, I, Persona, a social me, existed in the eyes of other people. Duped, dazzled, I did not hear the voice of the Great Computer joking: into the file girls, like accountants, whores, priests and artists, nobody's excepted, let's label you, number you, let's know what we're dealing with. We'll make do with appearances, we won't act nasty and peek behind the mask—choose a mask, quickly, any mask, and most of all keep it on your face *ad vitam aeternam,* never remove it; if your eyes aren't where the holes are, tough, yours is not to reason why, yours is but to die and die—what crap the computer was spouting, its buttons lighting up one after the other at a mad pace, such a grand old time it was having. Imbecile that I was, I said to myself: neat, they're asking for my input. I'm a Grown-up. I have been given the right to speak. Give me a break. I swelled up with this sensation of freedom and power to the size of a hot-air balloon, a poor jerk conditioned by my genes, stars, and bundles of complexes of a childhood I was laboriously recuperating from—in short, after this moment of ecstasy I began to wonder indeed what the hell I would be able to do later on since I seemed obliged to have some sort of idea. To sell *Le Figaro* on la Croisette, honest but not very ambitious. To play Ophelia, Agnes, Ondine, to call myself Lydie Laméra like my great grandmother, exciting but a trifle exhausting. Unless I became an Awful Floozy, a profession reeking of rice powder and Molinard perfumes. Teacher? Absolutely no way, educators were always badly rinsed off and smelled of powdered soap like the kind you get in train johns, whether it was a grade-school teacher or the specimen I had under my nose in the person of Mlle. Lipman, who was twisting her glass bead necklace with her white leukemic old maid's fingers and whose fox bolero stunk of mothballs —as far as furs went, I was going to have a whole slew, fluffy, glossy, curly, wild, rough to the touch; in a word, I would be a whore. That was settled; the only thing was that I felt this option wasn't exactly going in the direction expected of me. At any cost what had to be avoided was this abrasive frankness. Or else I would be off to lob bombs, blowing up emperors in their carriages, but sorry, there aren't any more emperors, the nihilists had disappeared with the last century, and looking all around me I really wondered who could ever replace them in this hopelessly humdrum world. By throwing my life into doubt because of this questionnaire, I came to the conclusion that even though radium, the cinema, the steam engine and penicillin had been discovered, and despite the disappearance of the nihilists, it might well be possible all the same that there still remained enough patches of jungle to explore, planets to discover, dictators to do in, languages to learn, and men to seduce to fill up this life while awaiting the next, as Genghivane had predicted while examining my palms, one of my last existences before fusion in nirvana, a reward that I had richly deserved, it was said, but which filled me with only a mixed happiness, for my contours were solidifying day by day like a vegetal membrane around my cytoplasmic Self; I was more fond of this embryonic envelope than anything else, and this immersion in the absolute only reassured me halfway; then Genghivane had to muster her every good intention to set my mind at rest and to assure me that, by becoming a part of the All, I wouldn't be disappearing from the surface of existing things only to melt into a nothingness full of delights, perhaps, but a nothingness nevertheless. You'll understand later on, she would say while pouring herself a shot of Mei Kwei Lun in a goblet no bigger than a thimble.

Time to hand in the papers, Mlle. Lipman said. In a panic, I snuck a peek at my neighbor on the right. Impossible to copy, considering her strategically bent posture. Lying flat on the table, nose level with her pen, her arm curling around her sheet, her hair falling down vertically like a curtain, she had enclosed herself upon a citadel of knowledge that she seemed determined to fiercely protect against any attack from without. If I tried to open a breach, a stream of boiling pitch thrown from atop the crenels was going to come down upon me. I gave it a try anyway and planted my nose squarely upon her form with the audacity of Suleiman the Magnificent laying siege to the walls of Vienna. The only

thing I was able to find out was that her name was
BÉCHEFIGUE Odette, and I told myself that that was just
what she deserved. Discouraged, I edged my slinking body
toward my neighbor on the left who, her duty done, was
daydreaming with her nose in the air while torturing the tip
of her pen, drawing up on it like a sucker, drooling on it,
nibbling it, sticking it in between her teeth, and appearing
to care as little about the questions asked as about the
answers to be given. As for her future, LARBAUD Apolline
Gisèle Jacqueline, born in Paris, ninth arrondissement, June
5, 1948 (shit! that made her nearly two years older than me;
to reach thirteen-and-a-half in sixth grade, she must be a
champion at being held back . . .), seemed not to give a
goddamn about it even though she had written in large
letters on her form: I WOULD LIKE TO BE A LATIN
TEACHER. Just to get it over with, coming back to my first
idea I scribbled without conviction: *actress,* and I was going
to put down my brand-new pen when I felt the widened
eyes of Larbaud land on my sheet. Are you nuts? she
whispered. Put what I did, Latin-Greek teacher's even better. Get moving, here comes Lipman.

So I deleted my future with two strokes, confirmed in the
intuition that it was best to let taboos lie in peace and that to
follow the path of my disorders, all I needed to do was to
pretend to follow the path of order. In one stroke Larbaud
Apolline had ushered me into the blurry, shimmering,
poisonous world of lies. As for our own, the world of truth
as bloody as a slice of roast beef, it had to be stashed somewhere to preserve it; otherwise they would have shoved it in
a trashcan or given it to the dogs, and we were still too small
to prevent this disaster.

The next day, Larbaud's seat was empty. Larbaud absent,
Béchefigue definitively padlocked in her silence like
Papageno, I had no choice but to lend an ear to Mlle.

Lipman's gibberish as she attempted to explain to us the origin of words. I learned that the Germanic invasions of the fifth century had left us *burg, beech, war, belfry, banner* and *warren,* words that were harsh, metallic, heavy, stagnating in a mist of blood; that *stern, wrack, wave* and *sail,* in the surf, undulating like sea gulls, had sliced through the seas to arrive on the continent with the Viking drakkars, while *algebra, camphor* and *admiral* ran like bands of Kufic calligraphy around the cupolas of Islam, and that from *apricot* and *mahogany* rose the intoxicating fragrance of sunny fruits and Macassar wood. Having to go up to the blackboard for exercise 39 was more of a hassle: use the following adjectives in sentences illustrating their meaning: *preventive, oppressive, compressive; jocund, rubicund, moribund.* The bell rang, with Polline never showing up, from which I concluded that she was sick, that I was sad, and that the key to words was good for nothing.

At noon, before going back home, I went to get bread at the bakery, across from the Saint-Vincent-de-Paul Church. While I was rummaging through my pockets for some change to pay for my half-baguette, with a nice shape and not too well done, I felt one of my toes being stepped on and was getting ready to let out a vehement yowl when a small five-limbed starfish instantly opened up as high as the left lobe of my heart. It was Polline, swaddled in an enormous plaid scarf that circled her head and dropped in a loose flowing tail to the belt of her curly wool coat, and there I was, forgetting about the two rolls of licorice I had snitched in passing and which were dangerously swelling the pocket of my peacoat, dumbstruck with happiness, convinced that I had closed my fist on the Double I had been trying to track down for quite a while along walls at twilight, as mystified as Narcissus believing he had trapped his non-existent love whereas he was merely pursuing his own warped reflection

—I remained there, my baguette under my left armpit, planted like a vegetable before the ghostly apparition of Larbaud, whose nose was running so badly that the space between her nostrils and upper lip was taking on a violet tinge under a film of crystallized snot and vaseline— Larbaud had a whopper of a cold, out of proportion with her body, but she would survive, plus she was talking, which was a good sign—I'm Polline, your neighbor on the left, she was saying in a tiny, polite voice—but that was something I already knew, since witches always come from the left.

Faubourg Poissonnière, 31A, near the Passage Verdeau. Reassuring but moth-eaten carpets. Ancient elevator smelling of age-old piss, walls graffitied with peckers shaped like trumpets, horns of plenty, or banana phalluses.

—They're all a bunch of sex maniacs in this place. And I draw on some balls here and there, it gets the old maids wet, Polline said. I would've already gotten the old one-two if I had uttered one-quarter of the filthy words that flowed very naturally from her calyx-shaped lips, as if they were alexandrines, a biblical verse, a stream of honey, the roses come out of the mouth of the drippy princesses in Perrault's fairy tales. I had never heard so many in the space of five minutes, and in one snap they lost their aura of sacrilege, their hellish flame faded until they became ashen embers, a timid scarlet brood with just enough heat to warm your fingers—they had such a flavor of authenticity, those coded words that neither I nor she really knew the meaning of, that while repeating them to myself in sheer delight on the landing I promised myself to learn some others, certain that I had discovered a vitamin-fortified language which finally stuck to reality.

—What the hell's she doing? Polline grumbles, ringing the bell a second time. She's scouring, scrubbing, polishing, she's getting it on with her O'Cedar broom.

—Who is?

—MY MOTHER. A fanatic about cleanliness. Oh here she comes. Don't goof up, use the floor slippers or else she'll yell.

The door crack opened, preceded by a sound of chains and sliding bolts. There's enough of them to last an hour, Polline remarks; she had a Fichet lock installed, but she still bolts herself in. On Sundays you could just as well kick off in front of the door before she'd open it. Oh it's you my little treasure, the maternal voice murmurs. Come in, come in. How darling your little friend is. You're just in time, I was making tea. A sideways glance at my feet already placed on the felt pads. Now there's a girl who has had a good upbringing. I take a gander at the parquet floor more shimmering than the one in the Hall of Mirrors, terrified at the idea of making a move in any direction whatsoever. Turnovers, I'm going to give you turnovers, before disappearing into a bedroom to emerge straightaway with two pairs of size 9 slipper-socks with leather soles. Couldn't you buy size 6, just for once? Polline groans while submitting to the ceremony with a grimace of weariness.

Later on, in front of the TV, Rin Tin Tin jumps from a roof onto an Indian's back and rolls with him into the dust. Poor Injuns, eaten up by those crummy dogs, beheaded by the thousands in the name of civilization and penned up in reservations like members of an endangered species. Let's close the parenthesis, let's get back to the present: in '62 girls rooted for Rin Tin Tin, and our noses in steaming bowls of Ovaltine, we were getting off something fierce—we, but me even more than Polline because I didn't have a TV, something my grandmother stubbornly refused on the pretext that it hurt a person's eyes. As a matter of fact, the TVs of that heroic time, with their wooden cases, their tiny beveled screens, their grainy black and white, were terrific pieces of shit, but all the same parading past upon this minuscule rectangle were horse races, Zizi Jeanmarie's legs, Typhoon Anita, and the political sideshows, in short the world set trembling by electrical convulsions and epileptic attacks—that's all the kids of my generation needed to split, later on, around the '70s, for unknown lands whose existence had been made known by Frédéric Rossif and the Mathuzier family—that's what TV was all about, about the unannounced entry into a slum in Pouceaux, Niévre, ten-thousand inhabitants, about Kennedy, Johnny Halliday and the cosmonauts, and a signal which one day projected thousands of children toward an elsewhere where they would not become agricultural workers or skilled laborers only to wind up alcoholic and doddering like the old man who, beret screwed down on his head, raised his elbow above the zinc of the grocery-notions-local bar of the village while swearing in front of his pals that he would welcome his offspring with blasts from his rifle if they were so unlucky as to show their faces because, don't you see, their mother hasn't come out of her room since they left and that, as for him, he has had his nose to the grindstone his whole life long so that his brat would become at least a foreman instead of going off to some God-forsaken place like Pizarro toward his Eldorado.

But for the time being, it was a question of Thursday movies and ladyfingers spread with butter, TV shimmered, crackled, blinked, fluttered in bichromatic mourning, and we treated ourselves to some great cocoa mustaches and pinched our arms when the sheriff arrived, whose eyes we guessed were inevitably blue, not knowing that in this month of October '62 the entire pack of kids our age who, their backsides riveted on chairs, were watching Rin Tin Tin flying into Cochise's feathers, already made up the next beat generation, the generation of freaks, of hippies and

leftists, the one which, while waiting for a kiss in a bubble
bath at Woodstock, were receiving smack-in-their-kissers
the festival of universal crapola broadcast by means of
images jittering frantically like the death throes of flies
trapped by a tooth mug.

*

Who will tell me if Polline, plunged into her Ovaltine, was
none other than my double, a projection of my darkest,
destructive tendencies, a vestige of an exorcism or a crystal-
lization of my awkward rage to live—and yet, faced with the
independent proofs of her existence, I am rather forced to
surrender to the evidence. If my father, Antoine Tristan,
practiced the profession of insurance agent, a respectable
facade behind which I suspected him of being a double
agent, Polline's, a gynecologist, had under his care all the
whores of the ninth arrondissement and particularly of
Pigalle, which permitted his daughter, from her earliest
years, to explore the neighborhood in a stroller, before
doing so on foot, under the protection of the professional
ladies who watched over Dr. Larbaud's offspring with keen
attention. Other proofs? Yes. Polline: your stolen perfume
(Molinard's Fawn's Kiss), your mentholated Hollywood
chewing gum breath, the anis color of your eyes, mercilessly
different from the autumn brown of my own pupils, slat-
shaped like the cap of Satan's mushroom. You're going too
far, you say, I'm staring at my navel. Don't get huffy, I was just
joking around, it really would have been a drag if I had found
no one to share the kingdom of five-franc moviehouses, the
boulevards, the squares, the candy shops, the Licorice
Palaces and the fantastic exhibition rooms of the Musée

Grévin—for that I needed some lucky devil who, like you, had received the power of changing into gold-bearing metal everything she touched, and the streams of piss of Pigallian gutters into torrents of nuggets as soon as you jumped across them with your legs together, a daughter of the moon and of the scorpion, a praying mantis chomping her chewing gum with the bold, choppy blows of her cruel mandibles, a magpie as stuttering and mercurial as the little subversive melody accompanying us from the Trinity metro exit where the sun was blazing as fiercely as at the doors of the Sahel, as far as rue Mauberge, to the Verdeau Passage and to 56 rue Pigalle where we took up our places in Bensoussan's cellar to ogle on the sly, through an enlarged hole in the wall, the beginning of the show at Chez Moune, and the transvestites' numbers, their lips embroidered in sequined blue, who by simply adjusting their paste-gem garters entertained us much more than the circus, a spectacle presumed to be for our age, the very idea of which made us absolutely suicidal.

*

If from far away Mme. Larbaud looked like she was thirty, seeing as how she was thin and her hair Venetian blonde, from up close you would have thought she was a child who had been cleverly aged with movie makeup, all frayed with fake wrinkles—I'd never seen so many before in my life on skin that covered so little surface, crow's-feet, the corners of her mouth, even her cheeks were embossed, incised, all craggy—but in the middle of this spider's web shone Mme. Larbaud's eyes, terrifying in their innocence, unbearable in their tenderness, like lookout beacons nothing could hide

from and which, in an emergency, she must have been able
to spin to the back of her head with one sharp jerk.

The unsettling sweetness of those eyes would have done
a number on me every time, but as for Polline, she had
escaped the spell long ago.

—Her affection, give me a break. She's always pulling
something on me. *Don't leave your mom all alone, she's the
only one who loves you, etc. Don't go out, it's raining and
it's dangerous, you can slip on the sidewalk or a chimney
might fall on your head.* My mom's completely nuts;
mentally, she's ten years old. Cuckoo. You know how she
spends her day? Sterilizing. Nothing escapes her rag soaked
with turpentine, her Lestoil and her wax.

Such a strange life Madame Larbaud had, her germophobia
driving her flat on her belly behind beds to hunt down the
slightest fuzz ball, and this right after finishing her house
cleaning, or methodically running her finger along the
edges of bureaus, along shelves or under armchairs with a
perverted and almost pathological patience, activities that
usually took up all her waking hours, when a sneaking
suspicion didn't pull her from her bed at night and send her
down into the kitchen where she threw herself into a hot-
headed rub-a-dub with the pots and pans, after which,
relieved, she went back up to lie down between impeccable
sheets which were changed every day.

This frenzy of cleanliness went hand in hand with a feeling
of wariness and loving hate toward objects. Arranging, clas-
sifying, labeling, stuffing into inaccessible cardboard boxes,
and in the end throwing it all away were the motor
functions of her existence. She lived in a perpetual bustle of
departure, as if the next day she was setting sail for Australia
or the afterlife, and nothing should be left behind after she
had gone, none of her Things (especially clothes and toilet
articles) on which she had declared war, tolerating only the

barest minimum which she nevertheless handled with the cautious respect due nail fetishes and other talismans an African witch doctor has empowered with a black aura. She said no to dresses, jewels and perfumes that spoke of sex, life, and ardor, and nothing filled her with a greater happiness than an empty clothes closet and a bare shelf. As soon as you spot something to throw away, she would say to Polline, be sure it goes RIGHT IN THE BASKET. Ten pairs of socks, what on earth can you be doing with ten pairs of socks? Look at this one, the heel's all worn out, you won't miss it. And there goes Polline, spending most of her time retrieving her stuff from the trashcan.

Nights, Madame Larbaud dreamed of an antiseptic, chlorinated paradise, of a universe as gloomy and deserted as those kinds of garages or sheds where a wheelbarrow dozes remembering the good old days, of a run-down shack where she wandered through a string of bare-walled rooms amidst furniture in dustcovers, with a gauze mask over her mouth like an Indian Jain who's afraid of swallowing a stray fly.

To hear Polline tell it, she washed herself three times a day from head to toe with a morbid fury, scrubbing her elbows and knees with pumice until they bled, as if she wanted to flay herself alive, until there'd be nothing left but a perfectly smooth skeleton, stripped of this scaly, fleshy and too easily infected substance: skin. What with all the Dermacide she shot up her pussy, said Polline, her vagina must be dry as tree bark. Nothing's splashing around in there anymore. Not one living cell, good or bad. Death to trichomonads. I wonder how she ever could have gotten pregnant. I'd rather be eaten away to a stump by smallpox and still feel alive than lead some long drawn-out ectoplasm's existence. Long live chancre sores, buboes, and pustules. We have all we want here, considering the number of whores with gonorrhea who come parading through my father's office—you can imagine my old lady's ordeal, drifting around on her ice floes in this ocean of gonococci. Not to mention my father's sadistic streak; soon as we sit down to eat he starts talking about the clap. . . . And whore stories, he's got a million of them. Terrific ones, too. Like for example in rue Quincampoix, the price range is between fifty and two hundred francs, dropping as you go down the street. Two hundred francs is at the very top. Young ones, who specialize. Then down to one hundred, still young, but no specialties, and then dropping to fifty francs, old bags, invalids, and grandmoms with goiter. At rock bottom there's Mlle. Hair-Curler. Sixty if she's a day. Always in hair curlers. The other day she went to have her teeth fixed at the clinic; they yanked out such a beautiful cyst that the med students decided to keep it as a souvenir, you know, to make a plaster cast of it. While waiting, Mlle. Hair-Curler's wandering around without her teeth and hoping the government will pick up the tab for her dentures—seems she's never been such a hit with the customers.

In the end I understood Apolline Larbaud, the Scheherazade of the sidewalk urinals. Faced with her mother's undifferentiated hatred for dresses, shoes, cosmetics, paper, pencils, tubes, bottles, vases, flowers, in short everything that proves you exist, confronted with this perpetual flight towards an airy Cytherean netherworld, she had no choice but to cling desperately to life by the roots, drawing crude penises on elevator walls, cursing with every breath, advertising her outrageous taste for pornography, stuffing her face with raw meat preferably full of germs, pissing in bidets, swearing she drank only fresh sperm, conjugating the verb *fuck* in every tense when she got punished with extra homework—I fuck, I fucked, I would fuck, I may fuck—a little joke which earned her her first

suspension, all the while remaining a virgin, trembling with
God-awful dread at the thought that one fine day she would
have to face the music and to be true to her philosophy,
she'd have to do more than immerse herself with me for
hours at a time in the medical dictionary while waiting for a
chance to get into a workshop. Speaking of the dictionary,
we would have loved to have gotten our hands on the latest
version but it was kept under lock and key in Monsieur
Larbaud's office. So we made do with the 1924 edition,
hoping that things hadn't changed too much since then.
What we learned from it, among other things, was that in
scholarly language pygmies were called achondroplasts and
had peckers twice as big as they were, that columbine made
you pee, wormwood tea set off your period, that there were
two categories of retarded children: the deaf-and-dumb and
the medical abnormalities which themselves were divided
into idiots, cretins, imbeciles, epileptics, and hemophiliacs,
that there were extended and double-sided harelips, and
anuses that defied nature, bifurcated or spur-shaped, that
puberty came from the Latin *pubis* (i.e., down), the first
signs of which were a flushed face, hardening of the nipples
and itching in the genital area—God, that was depressing
because we were on the pale side, our breasts were mushy
and unassuming, and if we felt like scratching anything it
was our calves or our ears, not our crotches, so this
delicious calamity was nowhere near befalling us; at twelve
I really didn't have too much reason to panic but for Polline,
who was thirteen-and-a-half, it was getting downright disturbing—and on the other hand, puberty had its dangers,
leading to manic depression, severe hallucinatory spells,
exophthalmic goiters and conjunctivitis with sties. But the
real treat was the entry under Female (from the Latin
femina). Poor sick animals. Must eat more often than men,
from which the custom of substantial snacks in the afternoon.

Are usually constipated. Piss less. Have varicose veins because of their garter belts and squashed intestines because of whale-bone corsets. Come equipped with a whole mess of inner gear, see chart, with tubes, twisting passageways, cracks, small lips and big lips, rounded tubercles, and at the very end of all these odds and ends a sort of squash, the uterus, which might find itself in a state of anteversion, retroflexion, anteflexion, or retroversion. To be honest, Mister Freud, what was happening on the boys' side held much less interest for us. Polline had a much better background in this area than I did owing to her father's profession and the care he had taken to put her in the know vis-à-vis life's realities the day he caught her in the basement being given a checkup by one of the neighborhood hoodlums, both pretending that it was just a kiddie game—but apart from the corny romanticism which made her flood of ignominious words so flashy, Polline worried as little as I did about the pecker problems boys our age had. Can you beat that, she would say, guys got five quarts of sperm to last their whole life, no damn joke, and here we were thinking of males as a kind of reservoir stopped up by a cork that was always on the verge of popping, no kidding, it's much better being a girl, *penis envy,* hoo-hah, psychologists crack me up, first of all it must be a pain to lug around, and anyway what was even more important than the theoretical curiosities of our adolescence was waiting for the moment when we would finally seize a fleeting glimpse of our own reflection magnified in men's eyes so we could hold onto it in the hollow of our hearts, consumed as we were with narcissism and self-love.

*

The most delightful moment of the week, the real treat, the epitome of pleasures, was eleven-thirty on Saturdays. I do mean eleven-thirty, on the dot. A gust of nonchalance passed over the class all of a sudden, an imponderable breeze of exhiliration, a zephyr of freedom that insinuated itself through the window chink. In a half hour's time the bell was going to sound the end of Latin class and the rush to the lockers; in front of us the Promised Land of Saturday and Sunday stretched out, but before that, the delectable instant when everything is possible. Mlle. Lipman might well get high on everything she knew about Greece the Mother of the Arts and ask us questions as perfidious as "Cur templa Romana altis columnis ornantur?"; she would garner nothing more than fragments of attention scattered here and there, even though the class seemed calm, the kind of calm before storms. We had our backsides lashed down on our room 34 chairs, but we were already someplace else. Mouth-watering expectation, a bit in the mouth, premises, promises, an indolent tenderness for all of creation turned my heart to putty, even for Bechefigue—poor kid, no Saturday-Sunday letup for her, she must have surely started churning out her homework as soon as she got in the door back home. On that particular Saturday, Schmauz's new socks, made of Scottish wool, had been drawing my eye since the beginning of class. They were genuine wonders to behold, those socks. And those Bally moccasins in red-brown leather, the color of the chestnuts gathered in the Cours-la-Reine, perforated at the tip with an imperceptible rosette. Tristan, continue. Naturally you don't know where we are. Hell, Polline says under her breath, page 98. Shit, I was still slipping through Greece. Hmmm. Ubi Pluto, mortuorum rex, sedet? Stupid question. Sub terra apud Inferos regnat. Estne feroci Plutoni conjux? *Ferocious,* the word is weak. Proserpine must be having a good howl over the censor. I see him now sitting on the serpent throne, trident in hand, while three-headed Cerebus ogles out of the corner of his eye, huge Charon, one hell of a strapping fellow, salivating at the thought of the cargo of the dead he is going to unload any second now and among which, perhaps, he will be bestowed with the privilege of munching a wee morsel, a bit of calf, a toe, or a piece of thigh on lucky days. Ten-to-twelve, whispers Polline, whose father has just given her her first watch. To climb out of Hell, all you need do is kick against the bottom like in the swimming pool when that jerky lifeguard has forced you to dive headfirst into the chlorine. I emerge upon the surface of the Acheron, splashing about in the muddy waters, ten minutes = six-hundred seconds, unfortunately so stuck to each other that you can't even pull off one with tweezers to glue it between the pages of a notebook and preserve it like a dried piece of edelweiss —no way to grab hold of the present, no sooner hatched than off it goes scurrying into the imperfect, it's already called future and becoming, but who cares? What matters is to try holding this reality in the future, a special time ought to be invented, a future-present, an indicative of hope, if for no other reason than this blessed half hour on Saturdays. The entire sixth grade is purring with pleasure; if Lipman wasn't so stone deaf, she would pick up on this indecent rumbling of happiness, and if she had eyes opposite her holes, she would catch stretches, yawns, and contortions translating a feline well-being, but all this sweet feverishness, this atmosphere of languid excitement seems to escape her completely, apud infernos she has gone off, down into the moist vaginal hole of the netherworld, embarked on the ship of the dead with an ample provision of gerunds and deponent verbs.

Five of twelve. Bensoussan slips me a handful of pistachios under the table. No, thanks, I won't be hungry for lunch anymore—and Saturday is the day for leg of lamb, the soft, the brown-pink, bordered with carmelized fat, with very thin string beans, with no threads, a dark green almost black, a bit scorched and all runny with butter from Charente. Great grub was also a weekend privilege, because during the week we stuffed ourselves with fried whiting, noodles, gray steaks and potatoes called *golden,* good Lord, Eve herself would have wanted no part of these bland cotton balls colored a yellow so sad it brought tears to your eyes—I had only one idea in my head in the dining hall: cram as much of the chow as possible onto Polline's plate who systematically cleaned up everything that was found there, even my mashed potatoes, Uhlmann's as well, the ascetic, who did not want to weigh more than seventy-seven pounds (anorexia, the docs said), plus Bensoussan's who, because of her stubbornly blocked choledoch duct, always looked like she wanted to puke up her soul. The pleasures of Polline, at thirteen, had remained at the oral stage. Everything that could be licked, nibbled, chewed, chomped or swallowed round and whole worked just fine to satisfy her bulimic sensuality. Around eleven o'clock, she began to die of hunger and to suck her thumb like a chocolate phallus. When her father had given her some dough (fifty francs a month, more than the thirty I got), she transformed her bookbag into a supply sack stuffed with praline-covered nuggets, Toblerone, Nuts, and especially my favorite treat, Mon Chéri chocolate-covered cherries—one bite into this delicate creamy cocoa rampart, a sugary, alcohol-spiked liquor set your palate on fire, and you had to suck very hard to get to the cherry—and that really was the pit of the world, the uncreated itself, formless nirvana running down your pipes.

To tell the truth, the whole class, fed on beans, was cooking up gastronomic dreams beginning at eleven on

Saturdays. But there wasn't only the grub. No way. Holidays, time telescoped, a day and a half off, the white cut off from the black. At the time, we cursed the lycée schedule, we found the break too short, without knowing that once we left the barracks, much later on, we would begin to miss the structures of this world divided up like a chessboard, demarcated by boundary posts and borders, where the only game consisted of passing from the occupied zone to the free zone, that is, cutting courses and employing a complex system of cheating whose aim was to spare us to the utmost degree the slightest academic effort. Who will restore to us the certainties of a Manichean universe, one never questioned, hours of work and leisure clearly separated by the ringing of the bell; who will give us back the psychic tranquillity of slaves who only need to rise up against kindly flesh-and-blood torturers—it's because they adore dictatorships, mankind's little ones, as soon as they begin walking on their hind paws; consider Nazism, the Boy Scouts, the kind of resorts dubbed "vacation" and *The Story of O.* They make a puddle of joy over it, to be dispossessed of themselves, deprived of choice, without any responsibility, beaten and acting unruly; oh sure you can go ahead and spank them as long as you take on their misfortune and their existential boredom, as long as you rid them of the dangerous happiness of living and of guilt, so that with perfectly clear consciences they may be able to lay the blame for the seed of every calamity upon the back of the schoolteacher, of the father, of capitalism, or of the Good Lord Himself.

I also accepted the cracks in time, and merely savored all the more the flare-ups of freedom which Saturdays and Sundays permitted us. That was all in the normal order of things. It's crazy how normal the world is for kids. Nothing surprises them. You tell them you're too little, you don't know anything; shut your trap, they shut it. You tell them you're not allowed to paint your bottom red or knock your teacher senseless with a tomahawk, they don't knock senseless and they don't paint. After all we might have protested, if only about little things to start off with, only about the fact that on Wednesdays they stuff us into a Green Line Bus stinking of gasoline to go catch the flu while gallivanting in small packs over La Courneuve's icy stadium, or declaring it useless to cram our brains with *rosa rosa rosam*—short of resorting to drastic measures and throwing everything into question simply by refusing, one fine day, to get up at the crack of dawn and deciding to stay in bed to gobble down croissants and to send flying in the face of the student prefects the dining hall's jellyfish stew—but no, instead of that we pretended to swallow down the Latin declensions, we tattooed our wrists with test answers and when we really wanted to loaf around we came up with diarrhea, bronchitis, growing fevers and spleen trouble, but all that was only rinky-dink lying, a pitiful transaction, a game for weaklings and cowards, an eternal compromising deal that we should have refused and instead convened parents and headmistresses in a general assembly and had them be judged by a court of children, and be condemned to death for abuse of power; then we would have been left to ourselves and never again would we have been bored to hell with deponent verbs, but the thing is, as I mentioned earlier, the happiness of life in the barracks is precisely that it doesn't leave any room for doubt and the fissures of neurosis since, while you're fighting a fascist power, you're not boxing with your inner demons who remain in peace and quiet down in the layers of the subconscious—so we made do with Saturday's delights at one minute to noon, accepting the infrangible boundary markers with which our illusory liberty had been flanked.

*

On Polline's left—that is, the extreme left—Bensoussan engaged in an ant-like industry. Never seen anybody busier than her. Multicephalic hydra, hundred-armed Kubera, in a minimum of time she managed to accomplish an incredible number of things. A prodigy of efficiency. A computer. On that particular Saturday, she finished her Latin-into-French translation that we didn't have to hand in for two weeks, destined betweentimes to be recopied on carbon paper and passed around the whole class; she sketched the course of the Danube with a blue pencil on a sheet of looseleaf, vaguely took notes on the countries of the Rhine and filed a whole pile of small pieces of paper that reached her hands from the bottom of the stack; Bensoussan lived at the pace of a Chaplin movie, allowing everyone the benefit of her genius and efficiency, which made her so popular that teachers, touched by the public rumor, always wanted to name her class president, a promotion that would have sounded the knell of her trafficking on the side, and the very idea of which gave her patches of eczema. Bensoussan's only gift was for organization, and the few talents she possessed were off the beaten track—for example, imitating the downstrokes, paraphs, scribbles, curlicues and other inky convolvuli whose complexities, resulting from the neuroses of our folks, posed problems for us when it came to reproducing their signatures at the bottom of a fake excuse note or a detention slip. Which explained the heap of accordion-folded papers accumulating in Bensoussan's desk drawer, her talent for forgery being combined with a meticulous sense of detail that later on would assure her a lovely career counterfeiting signatures for the owners of

stolen travelers' checks, somewhere between the Pudding
Shop and the Gulhane Hotel. But here I'm extrapolating;
Bensoussan in 1963 made do with preparing the *concours
général,* living on rue du Foin and getting paid in chewing
gum and other sweets, for if she reeled off irregular past
participles for the whole gang and lolled out her tongue
slaving over absence notes, it was all for apple turnovers.
When she got sick, panic swept the class, struck by a
genuine paralysis. Impossible to reproduce our mothers'
diagonal scratch marks, blotched and pointy like spurts of
bile spewn from the devil's mouth. Bensoussan had a thermometer stuck up her heinie and the shiver of her fever ran
through our bent-over backs. We blew our noses, we
sneezed, we spit for her, and when she made her reappear-
ance with her down jacket and her sealskin snow boots, we
dashed to the pastry shop to buy her a couple of pounds of
honey-flavored drops and chocolate mice to keep her
spirits up and so, most especially, that she wouldn't recatch
what her mother, using a discreet florid word, called a
coryza.

Below Bensoussan, floating in the ether of genius like
Sourya in her sun palace between two layers of clouds, the
plebes milled around, a magma that was simultaneously
gregarious, passive, racist and intolerant (*Ukatlic,* read: Are
you Catholic? the first question asked in gym class), already
presenting a sample of every human type: the sanguine, the
bilious, the phlegmatic, the melancholic, the nervous, the
excitable, the amorphous; I'll add the stubborn, the vora-
cious, the slogger, the paranoid, the schizophrenic, the
sluggard, the pathological liar—physically, as well, you
could categorize them, with just one glance at the Tourte
and Petitin photo, 1963. Thirty-nine budding blossoms at
the so-called awkward age—the age of Mercury, preceding
that of Venus, the acid age, the age of what is shapeless, what

molts and germinates, the age of the alluvial slime—rising in rows on a platform of chairs, the tall girls at the top and the little ones at the bottom, immortalized in all their glory in front of the clinic's blackish walls by the antique camera, equipped with bellows, belonging to Tourte, Petitin having been relegated to the printing because you never saw anybody but his associate who would descend upon us unannnounced, right on the day you had runs in your stockings, holes in your socks, dirt in your hair, or your acne erupted. Such a terrific gallery of ugly mugs. No need at all to bust your brain in order to see in place of these shapes a succession of zoomorphic heads set down plain and simple above the smock collars like those of calves' on the marble slab in butcher shops—and calves, that's what we were for the most part, but also representative examples of every feathery, furry or scaly creature in creation, even the vanished species, a genuine ark where old Poppa Noah would not have recognized his own, between beavers, pterodactyls with armed beaks, lemurs, anacondas, coral snakes from the Indies, marabouts from Java, rostrate whales, condors, blue foxes, gnus, the babirussas, the shrews—that's me, and owls—Polline. In short, an encyclo-pedic variety of every possible deformity on display right there like a living promise of suffering in all their imperfect disturbing truth, works of sculpture rough-hewn by the stiff fingers of a child-god who is ignorant of the golden mean and clumsy when fashioning human clay. Nothing but approximations, work that's unfinished, slapdash. And upon the surface, not a hint of that idealized veneer enveloping First Communion photographs where children's faces seem to drift amid the clouds, standing out against a blackish-brown mist which sends them at once to the heaven of abstraction, which discorporates them like the iconic figures lined up upon the opaque background of the chapels in Ravenna, not a hint here of the essential tricked-up studio lighting which transfigures the worst looking lump with the haggard eyes of a chronic masturbator into Bernadette Soubirous with an ecstatic gaze, polished angles, and an Ingres-like profile steeped in an angelic otherworldliness and immateriality. Not a trace of canonization at Tourte and Petitin's. The truth in all its rawness, gunned down in the cold gray dawn. Nothing but the secret and fragile substance, revealed in all its brightness, of thirty-nine countenances facing front, nothing but the harsh, transparent nakedness, blurred and washed out, of complexions that are sickly, grainy, scaly or gelled, dull as the white meat of a chicken, carefully scoured with soap—not the least background shadow to rub out the angle of the chin, not the least suggestion of pink to brighten the cheekbones, not a speck of powder to dim the cheeks, nothing but flowers without pollen, a lusterless frozen matter caught smack in the upheaval of gestation, but here and there. . . . Here and there a few points where the unforeseen essence had been concentrated, where the blind lightning of grace struck, bolts of the absolute scattered like gold nuggets at the bottom of a sieve, the murky seed of the disconcerting beauty of thirteen-year-old girls, a few faces of absolution and of charity, as dazzling as hosts or as ambiguous as masks, demonized by crescent rings under the eyes —here a dull stubborn forehead where the hair splits into symmetrical coils as rigorous as the Mayas (Mollet), there an undergrowth of Broceliande, a liquor of a look filtered through the overblonde barrier of the eyebrows (Uhlmann), the preserved vegetal pulp of a wet nurse's skin (Schmauz), the lips of a ravenous mandrake (Polline), pupils that are blue like the ultimate source of rivers (Berger), a gaze that is opaque, heavy, syrupy and Indian under a black butterfly-flutter of eyebrows (Papazian), and the untranslatable . . .

skinned knees, ivory knucklebones fit tightly together under skin turning blue, all bumpy from the cold, raspberry polish flaking off chewed nails, reddish-brown vestiges of a hot-tempered peroxide bleach job, the scalloped hem of a slip that is showing, the violet ink splotches at the tips of spatulate fingers, and in the midst of the magic spells of this suave adolescent wretchedness, between the owl Polline's chapped smile and the author's consternated scowl, hiding her legs because of the slightly fraying edges of her cotton ankle socks crumpled around her Giacometti calves, the teacher's eternal toothy grin captured in a wide-open bray.

Games in the Afternoon

In the lycée Lamartine we settled down for a long snooze off the beaten track, which the position of retreat we were to fiercely maintain for six years greatly facilitated, namely, the place between the window and the radiator in the next-to-the-last row, next-to-the-last since sticking yourself all the way in the back would only get you bumped from your seat at the first opportunity and separated from your bosom buddy thanks to the sadism of the teachers, obsessed with breaking things up whenever two kids hit it off. Wedged between the window and the hot pipes, I snored on peacefully, breathing in the fragrance of the chestnut trees in the springtime and following the basketball games with a placid gaze all the while hoping that the ball would come crashing through a pane and that dumb jerk Béchefigue, seated two rows further back, would get it right on the head, ruminating sticks of chewing gum or crunching pistachios, that is, whenever I wasn't all wrapped up in a feverish correspondence with Polline, blackening the margins (always the margin) of the *Aeneid* or the *Philippics* with a secret code stemming from ancient Greek and cuneiform writing, or in seventh heaven reading the Wedding Announcements of Mmes. Desachy and Butnar, or I wasn't taking part in one of those naval battles that mobilized the whole row along which the battalion of laziness was deployed; I picked

Papazian, the daughter of Armenian diamond merchants; Fisher, whose father was a furrier on rue d'Hauteville; Bensoussan, that underground girl Friday with a bevy of Crusoes; Leperron and Leperron-A, who still had a flip-floppy hand left over from her polio; Schmauz, called the Mole, because of the flat nose she got in a bicycle accident; Uhlmann, all flesh and bones, who looked like she was fed exclusively on unleavened bread and her inseparable Papovski; Mollet, a ward of the State adopted by pensioners; Nicolo, who only had one dream, the theater; finally myself and Polline in our duellists' act, even though at the time we looked more like Laurel and Hardy than the Dolly Sisters.

The parquet floor of the lycée had cracks and smelled of wax, an odor mingled with that of formaldehyde and ether when you got close to the science rooms. A little dose of ether and, whoops, time's turned inside out like a rabbit skin; you take your madeleines where you find them, and I find myself in front of this mouse bound and quartered on its cork board—go ahead, Schmauz, dissect or else I'll puke, I swear I'll puke—in front of a squid—are you going to pop that sack or what, God damn it! oh the awful rubbery ick, I'll never again be able to see that ink thing on an Italian antipasto table without turning my eyes away—or in front of a cow's eye soft as a custard—distinguishing the anterior and posterior ball-and-socket joint, the vitreous and crystalline humor.

The only thing that interested me in the program of studies, beside French, was life science class. I was to learn by heart and with sheer delight the composition of the retina with cones, rods, feasting on all that rigamarole about retinal purpura and night blindness, which I found far more poetic than alexandrines; the sophisticated organization of flowering plants and the study of a ligneous stem threw me into trances; the scars left by buds on the lenticellated bark of a beech branch or the traces of cotyledons on a string-bean stem bowled me over with tenderness. I went into deliriums before ducts bursting with sap, petioles, stipules, sticky buds, surfaces that were rough or smooth as velvety down, the close-packed felting of the piliferous zone of sweet-pea roots; all that chlorophyllic force simultaneously fragile and gentle fascinated me like a great organic festival. I spoke to plants in my dreams. I suffered with the flesh of flowers when I removed a piece to slide it on a glass slab and observe it under a microscope, but here, once my eye was riveted to the viewer, nothing in the world could make me budge. I stayed glued to the spot before the slow ebb of the turgescent vacuoles of a gladiolus petal or an elodea leaf, the muted red shimmer of lycopene crystals contained in tomato pulp, the slow current which drags the cyctoplasm along, a prisoner of its membranes, a fatal oozing that comes to an end only with the death of the cells. The vertigo of the microscopic, the activity of this deep life, flagellating, palpitating, the great waltz of the chromosomes made me giddy; I exulted whenever I had nabbed under my glass plate a polynucleated leukocyte or a buccal cell violently colored ultramarine by methylene blue; I gorged myself on the nucleic juice between the links of chromatine. I would have loved to make a bouquet of radiating asters and fix under the lens of my microscope the jellies, horns, spotted membranes, polar corpuscles, mucous matrix, flagella, all the fireworks and kaleidoscopic mirages of these moist asteroids, but they ineluctably escaped me, as fleeting as the exact instant phosphenes elusively explode under eyelids when you press upon them.

*

Aside from life science, we didn't learn anything about life in school. We were told lies. We were treated like real jerks. They fractioned us, rationalized us, divided the world up into samples. ANALYSIS in all its horror ran rampant. The obsession with dissection, the rage to nitpick around poets' hearts with a scalpel, a madness which has affected mankind from the fifth century in Greece to the present day, passing through the good old Cartesian eighteenth century. We, on the other hand, suspected that the truth was intuitive, something lived, and the world, activity and becoming, in which there existed antimatter and the square root of minus one, utterly irreducible to thesis-antithesis-synthesis. We still did not know that no sooner does a disciple ask Zen Buddhists a question and consequently enters the realm of reasoning reason, of duality, disassociation and death, than they whack his head with their staffs to subdue the useless mental commotion, but I had a good idea that all the theorems we dumbly recopied only to dry between the pages of our notebooks like dead flowers were pure relativity. Nevertheless, the universe shown to us seemed to rest solidly on its Euclidean pedestal, and the language spoken to us was fossilized enough to disgust us. And if it ever crossed our minds to dig down and discover the fissures of fire, they had painstakingly expelled the mischief makers from the culture proposed to us, silenced the mad poets, disincarnated writing and docked all drunken boats by eliminating in one swoop Dadaism, Surrealism, Lettrism, Apollinaire, Artaud, and Crevel, poof! all gone, even Rimbaud didn't get away unscathed, bound and quartered by the dreaded *explications de texte* that nearly succeeded in shattering the music of his words.

However, in eighth grade, Mme. Méry-Guichard appeared, sixty-five years old, with a heart condition, ah Mme. Méry-Guichard, the shadow of her long skirts brushing along the

sidewalk of the Faubourg Poissonière, the rancid taste of the
Breton cookies she offered whenever she had us over to her
place near the Gare du Nord, in her salon where the bronze
Bossuet of the clock, leaning with one elbow on the dial,
proffered his blessings to the roses under glass, to the velvet-
tassled curtains, to the so-called Dagobert armchair and to a
whole jumble of extinguished lusters, of old crumpled silks,
of iron candy boxes, a prewar world, a world of Pâtes la
Lune, over which reigned an Abyssinian cat who, traveling
backward through time like his mistress, dreamed of the
mythical era when she had a seat at the Court of the Dead
presided over by Mme. Méry-Guichard, in the form of Black
Osiris coiffed with the white miter of Upper Egypt, and
clasping against her heart the summons staff.

The first day of school, seeing this giant arrive swaddled
in a once-red fox, wearing skirts down to her ankle boots,
a compromise between Gunar, King of the Vikings, and
Harpo Marx, we were already offering each other our
deepest sympathy—then a miracle. This old mustachioed
trooper proved herself to be a genuine revolutionary who
taught us the subtle magic of poetical echoes and of free
verse, the sensuality of words—"wave piss of the moon-in-
chiffons, wave orgasm of the peacock-tail-sun" (that was
Saint-Pol-Roux), "feeling his good heart his heart of gold
sunk forever in this pool of poor gouged eyes immortally
lost in thought" (that was Jules Laforgue)—and Ophelia's
hair floated like jellyfish stingers in the pond at Elsenor to
the bottom of which Cocteau sank his plumbline, splash, a
matter of sounding the unconscious, while our dear friend
Diderot juggled with the galaxies and the millenniums and
discovered the notion of the unformed and the uncreated
some twenty-three centuries after Gautama Buddha.

Mme. Méry-Guichard confirmed our presentiments,
namely, that maya, the world of appearances, had to be

smelled, sniffed, touched, eaten, and drunk if a person
wanted any chance at happiness. Because as far as that went,
happiness that is, she was absolutely the only one to talk to
us about it. A taboo subject. We had the impression it had
never existed before us, so to speak. But it was breaking
resolutely on the horizon, it was rising like a sun upon the
closed garden of childhood, room 34 trembled on its
surface like a pond disturbed by a pebble; France was still
asleep, Louis-Philippoid, alcoholic, puritanical and pater-
nalistic, and we, beat generation in beige school smocks—
I'm especially talking about the next to the last row of the
class—we felt gusts of fresh air in the atmosphere that were
going to blow the dust off of everything; and even if the vice-
principal was still the only one to have a free hand, used for
holding our heads under lavatory faucets, for example,
while yanking our mops (Larbaud, I want to see a ribbon in
your hair and scour that face), our radars were not any less
attuned to the springtimes of the future.

But for the moment we made do with knowing that truth
was play. With Polline we mutually extracted the fantasies
from our brains the way you do pressing on blackheads. We
invented adventure, we unmade and recreated history, we
deciphered runes, we diverted the courses of rivers on the
Atlas with the mere flick of our fingers.

Mom and Dad Larbaud hadn't signed up their girl for
study hall, so as to all the better supervise her out-of-class
work, and she went home earlier than I, posting herself at
6:15 on her balcony where she waited for me to pass. That
winter, the one of '63, it was particularly nippy, it was a
good old-fashioned winter, the kind they don't have anymore, because even the seasons became part of the system;
it wasn't so long ago that November was still called
Brumaire, and for a good reason. We were cold for three
months long, we just had to resign ourselves. There was no

one yet who would upset the cosmic calendar so as to "turn around in the cage of the meridians" and seek out the heat of the Tropics at Christmastime. In short, we shivered while killing time outside of the classrooms before math because the teacher always arrived late, the tail of his Davy Crockett hat bouncing against his back. Our skin was peeling from the cold even before going into study hall in the courtyard where from five o'clock on a shadowy frost crept in with the same purplish hue as our numb icy fingers. But inside, in one of the oldest rooms of the lycée, the kind of room they don't make anymore, in multiple levels, with rotted tables where Polline drew pornographic graffiti that we would later erase with rice paper, all warm and comfy, barricaded behind our books, we started into the most charming part of the day, the chitchats-semistudy daydreams, while the student prefect, a fat Austrian nicknamed Sissi Goulash, was plunged in her detective novel and didn't lift her nose before the six o'clock bell, indifferent to the background hum inspired by passing around the Vergil translations bought directly from the bookstore down the street, not from the one across from the lycée at least, plus Schmauz's Cutex nail polish along with her emery board. Then we worked away, and what a real pleasure it was. At home, I had all the trouble in the world finishing an assignment, whereas there, in that ruin of a study hall where in wintertime low-hanging lamps were lit in the middle of the afternoon, diffusing a dull blue-green brightness that was as confidential and murky as that of certain poolrooms, there I managed, so I think, to cheerfully pump out my Latin or Greek translations out of sheer sensuality, because the smooth, round point of my pen slid along the icy Claire-fontaine paper with its imperceptible violet grid, and I got my fix, thanks to inhaling to the very bottom of my lungs the print odor of brand-new books that crack when they're opened and whose rebellious pages just won't lie flat and must be quelled—taming a book is like being in a rodeo, you mustn't make it afraid of you at the start but at a certain moment, use an iron hand—how I loved books already with such a love, but the kind that have been handled, dog-eared, torn apart by the reader's rage.

When six o'clock rang, Sissi Goulash shut her Hadley Chase and we dashed to hang up our smocks in place of our coats; in the empty courtyard the black sweeper, now only visible by the whites of his eyes, gathered the last dead leaves that rustled with a sound of crumbled calcium; there wasn't a smell of fried whiting anymore or the clatter of half-hinged toilet-stall doors, nor the muffled tap of the ball hitting the basketball pole, nothing anymore but the silence of the school in its sleep, only disturbed sometimes by the music coming from the direction of the phys-ed room where girls in black leotards were rehearsing *Giselle* and *Swan Lake* until after six. Then the gang—Leperron and Leperron-A, the one who had such pretty hair, natural ringlets, Schmauz, Bensoussan, myself and a dozen others—bundled up, in our rain hoods and ski masks, our teeth chattering, went down the stairs into the mauve cracks of the fallen darkness.

At 6:15, Polline arrived at my house, and we hid on the balcony, behind the shutters, equipped with a can of shampoo fortified with toothpaste and egg yolk, a concoction destined to land on the heads of passersby, plop on the back of the victim's skull, and with us two savoring the Chaplinesque way the scene was played out, almost working ourselves up into near seizures with our laughter, until the day when the mailman, all slimy, came ringing at my door to inform my grandmother that we were rotten sonofabitch

bastards, which she took as a personal insult and which got
Polline banished from the premises for two weeks.

Beside the shampoo ambushes, we had more intellectual
pastimes, for example, Battle of the Barbarians with bolsters
for weapons, Circus Games in which the retiarius had to
imprison the gladiator in a shopping-net bag while ducking
the lunges of her dreaded pillow, the Rape of the Sabines
personified—the whole bunch of them—by the cat we tried
stunning with our bolsters before cornering it in a hissing
rage behind the armchair so as to shut it up in the hamper—
and what he let fly in the way of insults, that obnoxious,
lucifugous creature, you forget, he growled, that I am the
Carthusian Cat and a half-dozen times over have I gathered
your feet cut off in two pieces, by my whiskers you'll pay for
this, all right so I'm a castrato but that's no reason to take me
for a Sabine and cram me away in this awful hamper, anyway
I know this witch who keeps a herd of toads out by the Saint-
Cucufa pond and we'll see who has the last laugh. . . . So to
calm him down I had to knead his spine, I had to massage
the nerve center where, at the cerebellum, in a small bulge
of fat was located the nexus of his unique voluptuous
pleasures, I had to chop up a little bit of steak dipped in
brewer's yeast or, failing that, squeeze some sweetened
condensed milk into a saucer. We would have given
anything for this milk as sticky and white as a shooting star's
sperm; we extracted the last drop from the tube, squeezing
until it was no more than a crumpled accordion and our
teeth came up against metal, desperately sucking in the
residue of the Nestlé ambrosia, but all our tongues got was a
little bubble, tasting of sweetness and a disappointing
metallic saliva.

Our most erotic pastime was Cleopatra's striptease, for
which we tacked up the living-room curtains in such a way
as to form a wigwam under which the most exhibitionist of

the two, depending on the mood of the moment, her eyes smeared with Caran d'Ache and a Scotch tape band on her forehead, ornamented with a uraeus cut out of the columns of *Ici Paris* that heads of lettuce came wrapped in, threw herself into a Dayak war dance that had not the least thing in common with the lascivious rolling hips of the Egyptian woman whose nose held such a powerful fascination for us.

*

If Saturday afternoons came racing down the sides of the Himalayas with the force of a thaw torrent flooding the jungle of oaks and screw pines, Sundays swelled to the dimensions of a genuine typhoon, especially those blessed by baby Jesus when Polline's parents—having gone off to their country house in Bailleul near Beauvais, Gallic capital of the Bellovaques—left us alone in the Faubourg-Montmartre apartment which for me possessed three intriguing elements: wall-to-wall carpeting, a Chihuahua that always looked ready to kick off at any minute, and the most enormous TV I had ever laid eyes on, in front of which we spent muffled afternoons consecrated to subversive activities, like sitting on the floor to eat our Quiche Lorraines and cream puffs from Bourdaloue's instead of the chicken, peas, and rum cake of real family dinners that dragged out until four o'clock, and romping around in PANTS, the very symbol of freedom, forbidden in the lycée except for ski pants on days it was freezing. Unfortunately, an obsessive whim began to run through the heads of Polline's parents: having us breathe good air, that is, the carbon dioxide put out by the exhaust pipes between Paris and Beauvais. Try as we might to object that there were too many car accidents and that we puked in motion, and that, and that, nothing worked. No choice but to let it happen, at least once every two weeks. We knew intuitively that if we let ourselves be sent off to Beauvais twice in a row, we would be done for afterwards, because parents always go in for habitual activities, got to keep them going at the same rhythm, never leave them any time to catch their breath, when they're doddering it's the same thing, if you go see them once a week, Wednesday let's say, absolutely out of the question to set foot in their door once on a Thursday, otherwise they won't have had what's due them and the next week they'll ask you to come back both days.

Conquered by the coalition in the end, we stuck out our Sundays in Bailleul, absolutely swearing each time to disgust them with our presence. The weather, it must be acknowledged, generally was our ally. That is to say that, leaving at nine in the morning sticky with sleep, we arrived around eleven smack in the middle of a pea-soupy fog in a deserted village planted with bare trees; never saw anything as mournful as Bailleul, even the sunshine, whenever it tried to break through, turning the walls more scabby and the grass more yellow. Pop Larbaud had not even turned the key off in the ignition yet when, already alerted by the sounds of the motor, all the curtains trembled with excitement behind the jalousies, what a beautiful name that is, jalousies, I heard the sound from here, creaking between their slats: Hey here come the Parisians to patch up their dump, wouldn't they be better off back home where it's warm instead of coming out here making a damn nuisance of themselves, but did you get a look at their getups, the curtains murmured, where's the old man going, with his sewer worker's boots, no trout to catch in these parts. And those girls, pale as farts, that's Paris air for you, and the expressions on those ugly kissers, but honestly they carry on like princesses, those little snotnoses.

After which we parted the nettles and went into a house rotting away from dampness and half tumbledown—where everything needs to be done, M. Larbaud would say avidly. First off, weeding and replacing the roof tiles; second place, finishing the wall at the back of the garden and planting something in that garden—Yvonne, I hope you've remembered the seeds; third place, interior decorating. And M. Larbaud began to cut wood enthusiastically, quite a heaping pile of logs, because you needed at least two good hours to warm up one single room; when we were on the point of leaving that's when it started to become livable, but in M. Larbaud's defense I must admit that he really did everything in his power, but those wood fires of Beauvaisis have rotten characters, they start crackling cheerfully, sputtering, spitting sparks like the crater of Gunung Batur, then mysteriously become dormant, huddling in the hollow of the branches, coiled like boas with incandescent skin, before dying out for good. Fudge, M. Larbaud would say, vexed but polite, I'm going to have to go fetch some logs, girls come give me a hand, and from that point on things would start to go all wrong because M. Larbaud had a sense of self-esteem and his battle with Fire ended up by taking on Homeric dimensions; he forgot all about eating; he could hardly take a nap once he suspected that the enemy, settled in the bottom of the fireplace, started to play dead again. Food was another problem. A major enterprise consecrated to a piddling result. Go to the market, M. Larbaud would say, always keeping one eye on the fireplace, until this damned wood fire starts roaring I'm not setting one foot outside.

Going to the marketplace might have had a quaint appeal to it, but Saturdays it closed early and we always got there too late when all that was left was kohlrabi and pork chine. Or else veal. Veal goes very well with hick towns and parents. It's something innocent, veal is, it's white, it looks completely drained of energy, it makes for good hospital fare, and red cabbage especially with endives, nothing sadder as vegetables go. We ended by having lunch. After lunch, the dishes. After the dishes, naps for the exhausted parents, while we grabbed an umbrella and took a stroll along the road; even the cows had a laugh watching us go past.

Around five we came back for tea. M. Larbaud in a sweat pushed his wheelbarrow full of rubble found in the empty lot on the side, destined to separate off the back of the garden by a symbolic Maginot Line whose flanks would remain open, but it was all the same *his* wall; the French have always gone in for that sort of thing, having their little piece of ground, remember my late grandfather with his bench in Nemours, the only difference was that here the project proved to be somewhat chimerical given the rate of ten bricks a week that M. Larbaud dared not exceed due to his high blood pressure and the fact that not one of the women present volunteered to help him ferry around those clumps of muddy blocks in the rain. In spite of everything, M. Larbaud was generally delighted with his day, and whistled the whole way back while in the rear of the 403 we alternated fits of sneezing with nausea and rhonchus, which might have been for real what with burnt veal cutlet, the odor of Super Shell and fresh country air, the very memory of which made us shudder with horror come Monday mornings.

Mens sana in corpore sano, said M. Larbaud, who loved speaking Latin so much—if the Sunday bouts of back-to-naturitis represented health, we preferred to kick off suffocating in the stale air of the Rex movie house and the pollution of the boulevards, and besides, curiously enough, concrete and the dust of Paris were the only things that suited us physically; we drew our strength from the asphalt like Antaeus from his mother Earth, and from the pavements that bore us along like moving walkways to the very heart of the city.

Easter 1963. The attic where I am staying with Polline at my aunt's camp-hotel in Touques-Trouville. An odor of dampness and suntan oil. Polline in a two-piece bathing suit striped sea-blue and white, coats herself from head to toe with a brownish grease, a concoction that reeks and costs an arm and a leg; later on we'll move on to buckets of cream from the udder, but for the moment nothing beats Helena Rubenstein for the price. She pours out a small pool in the hollow of her palm, gives it a stir with two fingers and sends gobs flying every which way—Polline in profile against the window, outlined with a fluffy garland of sunshine, as polished as Balinese wood, all the darker under the brilliant coat glazing her skin beaded with a very fine sweat, turns around and pulls on the stretch band of her slip to show me the line as precise as a scar separating, below her belly button, her burnt-crust tan from the dull pallor of a sickly secret winter skin that doesn't look as if it belonged to her anymore. You see the results after two days? she says triumphantly. How about going down to the garden? I saw your aunt leave for the marketplace, that gives us a solid hour of peace. Wait, I'll do your hair up in a bun. And with one flick of her hand she gives my hair a twist at the top of my head, knots it in a kind of tight knit that she holds in place with two golden pins with a dexterity that will always

be beyond me for want of having taken classical dance
lessons as she has, which aside from art and how to tie up
hair in buns, taught her the freedom of movements that are
flexible, long, continuous, a constant harmony fixed at
times in perfect poses struck with the tragic seal of ineffable
grace.

Now I've done it, freckles! I said while discovering my
second face in the mirror, my vacation and summer disguise,
my ball mask of brown splotches covering my nose and
cheekbones, and reaching all the way to the fragile corners
of my eyes. The bewitching sun had already begun to work
its metamorphosis, smoothing angles, softening the skin in
those places where it allowed the dry imprint of poorly
ossified bones to show through, bleaching our hair—such a
sad auburn under the Paris sky—like a clever dye, brighten-
ing it with gold filaments like those princesses abandon on
purpose on the edges of wells so that knights may quest the
whole world over for them. Collapsed in striped-canvas
lounge chairs, velvety all over with the sun's pollen, Polline
and I savored a moment of calm stolen from an existence
devoured by the immaterial demands and feverish longings
of our bittersweet age, the age of phosphorus, of patholog-
ically hopeful mornings and disappointed evenings, the
futile debilitating comical age, the age of half-portions, half-
smiles, between day and night, the arctic dawn of age
thirteen, a mirage deep in the great *kavirs,* pathetic
rainbow, tarnished beauty, pearls before swine on account
of being underage, not listened to, not looked at, non-
existent, and yet the key to the world exists in a tube of
mascara and of lipstick; all it takes is a hint of black on the
eyelash tips, some sparkly doodoo around the eyes, a streak
of eyeliner, a strand of color on the lowered eyelid that you
draw onto your temple with a finger and presto! here we are
transsublimated into witches, even our bone structure

changed, and our smiling kiddy faces are mere receptacles for a Hindu dancing girl's eyes. If only I didn't have this nose, this damned nose, Polline complains, denting her straw hat with a punch. A nose like yours is a real crime. You ought to have to pay taxes on a nose like that. It's not there, that nose of yours. It's a sink hole. Just come right out and tell me I look like a monkey, I say, turning on the transistor. Dummy, she says, and so what do I look like? A toucan. A buzzard. An owl. I've seen schnozzes like mine on Mayan reliefs. Who's to blame? My father's side, meaning one day he clubbed me so hard that the septum got thrown out of whack.

Hey, that's a new one. Compulsive liar, that Polline, it'd surprise me if her dad beat up his only child. Uh, well, I said, I've got a double ankle. Look. Two bones. Because my mom slammed me with her foot, she has kicking fits now and then.

Oh really? Polline says skeptically, desperately rubbing the little bump which gives her nose the slightly hooked line she hates so much—the only defect and the greatest charm of her Florentine child's face. From the front, classical, Greek, Botticellian perfection; in profile . . . in profile, my bird of prey, my priestess of Quetzalcoatl, my plumed serpent, that tiny bone jutting in a place where it's least expected makes you look a little cruel, stubborn, head-strong—the air you have of a vulture or nighthawk, your air of violence belied by the vulnerability of your lips as fleshy as the inside of a tulip calyx, which even when closed look open, your Negro girl's lips whose delicate flesh deepens to a dark purple when the blood rises in your cheeks and in a fit of rage you sink your nails into the palms of your hands (I've done it now, I'm bright red, I feel it, my face is tingling to the roots of my hair), has anyone ever seen such a mouth, the upper lip slightly puffed in the center by a tiny roll of flesh like Akhenaton's, the madman of the sun, the lower as swollen as a muscat grape, a whole well-ripened field, a juicy bunch ready to burst, your lips a wound of love, a bruise, a secret scratch, an opening to a head-spinning world, scarlet membrane of the carnivorous rafflesia, insolence and shamelessness, when you run your tongue along it it's as if you're brushing past your genitals, respectable people ought to bury their faces before such a scandal, you know it and your parents ought to realize it and forbid you to look at the assistant butcher that way, surprised eyes, lips slightly drawn back over the barrier of your moist teeth, and force you to go out hidden in a veil like an Arab woman or to tone down with makeup foundation that provocative gash which can also become a smile that's so intense it's almost ugly, wrinkling your bumpy nose, rounding out your face until the chiseled shadow of your cheekbones is forgotten, and crinkling your eyes until they look Chinese and only a starry trembling is visible between the crack of the lashes, then your mouth opening on the rather obscene secret of your gums and the roots of your incisors is neither sexy nor perfect anymore but it doesn't matter to me, it might just as well look like two slices of raw steak, I'd gladly run my finger along it to taste the tartness of the green apple you've just bitten into, and I'd scoop up the discoloring core to turn it into a precious relic like the Holy Shroud, stamped for all eternity with the precise corolla of the irregular and sacred imprint carved out by the enamel of your teeth.

*

Looks like the weather's turning lousy, says my aunt Roberta, called Ro. Now you help me take in the laundry, the lounge chairs, and the beach umbrellas.

Time's over for getting tanned, the transistor, the wasps, and our eyes mint green because of the sun. Bowed under the weight of a beach umbrella and a half-dozen terry-cloth towels, I give Polline the wink of secrets, whispering in her ear: Take in her wash without any lip, and wait and see what comes next.

What came next was pedaling along the Deauville road supplied with ten francs each for the movies, permission granted by Auntie because of Easter, the rain and her desire for some peace, with the orders not to go strolling on the boardwalk to get ogled by guys, a prohibition purely for form's sake and whose aim was to bring Ro into accord with her conscience.

My aunt or going out. I loved my life in Touques because it was made up of a series of small gifts. It slipped along, it flowed all by itself, you had all the elbow room you wanted. Back home I was constantly running into a gigantic No. The thin air exclusively condensed negative atoms. No, no no and no, you won't go see *West Side Story,* you won't read Françoise Sagan, you won't wear stockings at age thirteen, I'm telling you to take off that eyeliner, you come to the table on time, etc. Refusing was what parents were put on this earth to do. I wondered how, so conditioned, they had been able to say yes at least once in city hall. The world of adults was a No with a capital N, and the Yes's existed only in my dreams. Now that's where things went just great. Yes yes yes yes. . . . From Thomassina Thumb, no bigger than a pea at the foot of the tall buildings of NO, made of steel, glass and concrete, I became the Princess of Yes moving in an affirmative universe where I passed between a double row of affable courtesans brandishing signs painted with big red letters: OUI-DA JAWOHL YES SI OF COURSE, to bow at the foot of the throne of my father King Jawohl while a herald arrived to take his place behind me, unfurling a roll of parchment as long as a carpet and reading in a resounding voice my petitions for the week, to which the king acquiesced with a tender nod of his head—besides, most of the time he sort of lost track of things, fell asleep in the middle of the list, then regaining consciousness startled awake on his throne as if his fingers had just been jammed in a socket and shouted: stop, stop, it's all right, it's all arranged, I consent, of course, you'll have it, okay, you'll get your way, obviously, you're right, it's understood, it goes without saying, naturally, it stands to reason, anything you want, I agree, I beg you take my daughter away, her herald and his parchment or else we'll all be here until dawn.

The Touques camp-hotel resembled the court of King Jawohl, the same leniency, the same atmosphere of compliance, the sliding doors closing and opening silently like the eyes of cats; we spoke in hushed tones, we sang, we ran our hands wrong-way against time's fur, and time let us do with it whatever we wished. My aunt's Yes generally preceded a *but,* real tiny, itty-bitty, a *but* that was affectionate, inoffensive, something to take the guilt away, a *but* for appearance's sake. But don't go on the boardwalk, Ro would say, for whom the definition of Deauville was contained in a few words: a casino, hookers, and a wind "to blow the horns off a bull." Her Normandy, which had nothing in common with this tainted, polluted place, to which she nevertheless owed the success of her campground rented by tribes of M. Hulot fascinated by the lights of the coast without having the means to put themselves up at a palace, covered an area between Caudebec-en-Caux, Touques, and Etretat, where she came into the world, grew up and married Leon Bouju, a hotel keeper's son, whose grand ambition was to start up a campground near Deauville, where Bouju, once settled inside his walls, lost no time in kicking the bucket (under mysterious circumstances), which made Aunt Ro the sole uncontested directress of his Norman estate, a situation she took to so quickly, thank you, that the family harbored a few suspicions as to the real cause of her spouse's death.

Aunt Ro, born under the sign of Aquarius, incarnated the Chinese principle of the Yin, of the hollow, the dark, the moist and the fluctuating, most likely due to her innate character but also thanks to a slow osmosis with the country-side, for as a result of living in the rain between two drafts she had taken on the look of a large wall blister brought on by dampness and seemed to condense every shower falling on the so-called Jade Coast in the dripping frizzle of her weeping willow hair, her washed-out, transparent pupils, and her swollen nose reddened by a chronic cold caused by her fondness for garden strolls at the crack of dawn, all naked under a wisp of nightgown falling open on breasts shaped also like drops of water.

She permanently resided under her personal drizzle, a microclimate where the wound of sunlight never came to rummage through her fragile Lady-of-the-Rain eyes, upon a damp colorless planet made of quartz, a country of floods and frost, a pearly moonscape where the only games were played in water; she clapped her hands and the thunder of the Iguacú Falls resounded at the same time as the revolving mist from the sprinkler gently hissing on the grass, and to us she willingly abandoned the daytime world, the brutal, boldly outlined, garish world of the Yang with its green chlorophyll and stupid yellow sunshine, as if the country around Touques, transformed no sooner than a guilty ray crossed the cumulonimbus into vivid Manet whose flat spaces were silhouetted in black, left her but one possibility: to hide away in her room, draped in her nightgown as in a threadbare toga to check over her accounts for the hundredth time, while waiting for the world to become suitable once more, liquid, shaded in grays, fluid and shimmering like a Sisley painting.

My aunt of vapor, of mist, of fog, of dew, of hail and of monsoon, evaporated in the sunlight like a small puddle but, no sooner did she disappear than she regained her strength, making her way up to our rooms to see if we were moving along with our holiday assignments, a symbolic effort that put her out as much as us but set her mind at ease, after which she disappeared once more. We saw her only rarely, not even at mealtimes, for contrary to other grown-ups who always looked haggard, racing around like the March Hare once he had swallowed his watch, this nebulous aunt would completely forget everything that had anything to do with schedules—in the kingdom of Jawohl people didn't have the slightest inkling as to what such things even were.

My aunt, as light as a scarf of fog, had rainbow-tinted bursts of affection now and then which took us by surprise all the more since the rest of the time she didn't seem to grant us one iota of attention. She prepared teas for us that were exquisite, immaterial, worthy of dear old Mme. de Ségur's little lace-trousered namby-pambies. Pure dream teas, for which she brought out her Limoges set and an extraordinary ribbon-noodle teapot, as ornate as a pumpkin that remembered it had once been transformed into a car-riage. And while we lapped up the barley syrup milk and the Chinese tea—from Great Yunnan, children, it's given to surgeons before operations to help them concentrate—and scraping what was left of the caramel custard at the bottom of the fluted porcelain ramekins, we savored this incredible infraction of the laws of a world that forced us to feed ourselves at one o'clock and at eight no matter what our bellies might think, and we drew the pleasure out to the maximum degree with the thought that tonight at ten we would come down and snitch a piece of Gruyère and an apple from the fridge without anybody having it in their head to rivet our bottoms on a chair or our mothers' fatal TIME TO EEEEEAT resounding at the end of the hallway, which made us topple from our dreams without any time to unroll the silk ladder.

At those times my aunt watched us eating up her petit fours with the attentive, quizzical look of a zoologist before a pair of horned vipers. What did people call those hybrid things, those undines, those manatees writhing about, putting on airs? They're real cute kids all the same, she would tell the cook. And so calm. You never hear them. Studious too. Obviously they paint up their eyes to look older, but that doesn't hurt anybody. And dear Yvette (my mother), who's worrying herself sick that they're going to hang around the boys in the campground. No such thing. I see them myself in the morning going past with their deck chairs and their cooking fat, they hardly even glance at the customers. Like real duchesses. But I'm telling you my sister and her conniptions . . .

And she smiled imperceptibly, under the mustache that made her look like a seal.

—You can bet she'd have a good laugh if she found us in our room with some boys, Polline said. Maybe she'd pretend to get all worked up, but just for form's sake, the old hypocrite. Behind those scatterbrained airs that aunt of yours is a shameless old hussy, that's why we understand each other.

A hussy, maybe not, even if she poisoned her husband, it could only have been done absentmindedly, a little pinch of arsenic in passing, an altogether convenient crime that put nobody out. With that moist smile and those washed-out eyes, how was it possible to believe she could experience the vivid red of hatred? And yet, from time to time, my aunt got back her color, and her dampness condensed into huge pearls like those that roll along rose petals. Then we saw that she must have been, as common folk say, *appetizing*. She would have us sit by her side and she would tell us kind of crazy stories that always had to do with a lost dance card, because of which she had missed *her* dance with the man she loved, and I, charmed by the poetry of this story for love-sick secretaries, I drifted away on waves of Strauss while Polline, not smothered by ethereal romanticism, shrugged her shoulders as she stuffed herself with Lajaunie cashews.

The Boardwalk. A mythical forbidden path. Lewd sun, tinny glint on the ocean, dull snow reflections on the cold sand, the red spindles of folded beach umbrellas; look, Polline, look in the distance, that ghost sardine boat against the colorless sky, and over there those horses galloping on the beach—it's as if we were above, we feel the wind biting our cheeks, depositing a violent taste of salt on our lips, squint and you'll see beyond the horizon the tropical atolls and at the bottom of the sea the digitate shrubs of coral reefs —the world has no boundaries. Polline my Mayan priestess, and it's the black horse team of freedom passing within hand's reach, we have only to leap on it in mid-gallop like the stuntmen in Westerns.

—So, no kidding, there's really NTJO round here, she says to me while casting a heartbroken glance at the deserted Boardwalk Bar.

—???

—Nobody to jerk off, she stoops to clarify. Yesterday the assistant butcher said to the Blondin's maid that he wouldn't be *jerked off* by some old reactionaries.

—Oh, I say in an uncertain tone, giving up the idea of asking for any explanation before her air of satisfaction, which would have made me come off like the dumbest dumb bunny.

At which point a grandpop taking his poodle out for a walk passes by us and murmurs above his muffler: Oh such pretty little chickies. . . . Polline about-turns, spits on the ground Indian style and wails: Go jerk off someplace, you old sadist! before tearing off like a zebra dragging me along by the hand. Considering that ugly face of his, she tells me, he must be just wild, but I REALLY haven't the slightest idea what she's talking about.

*

Easter vacation came to an end. As I saw my aunt's silhouette drawing away into the distance on the train platform, I knew I was leaving a world that was gentle, permissive and poetic to return to the shrunken universe of my thirteen years, and I felt a lump in my throat. My aunt simply forgot that we were children. What's more, she couldn't have given a damn. She loved us like her roses and her cabbages, to which she now and then flung some water from her swaying can a little late; things were growing, not growing, growing up all crooked, just leave nature alone to do what it does and God only knows that for our part we asked one thing only: to be treated like her flower beds. But already the rainbow in the distance clouded over and with it the rain's smile disappeared.

The day Polline showed up in school wearing a so-called *madison* skirt, in houndstooth, pleated in the front, a black T-shirt and flat cyclist shoes with golden eyelets, I forgot to pass along the Krunch Bar that we traditionally ate in geography class (what am I still hearing? Uhlmann, get up and go spit it out, do you hear me?). Without fail, Uhlmann was the scapegoat, and we could keep Krunching, krrr krrr a tiny sound, unspeakably nerve-racking, that coupled pleasure with danger, like the cracking of pistachio shells and the dribbling burst of chewing-gum bubbles; I forgot, as I was saying, to break my square off in passing and I let Bensoussan help herself to my share. Polline, that bitch. She arrived late on purpose, her blouse open. And stockings, well I never, her first pair, champagne colored, a little wrinkled at the knees, but what do you want? Like the burning bush, that outfit. And Polline was as radiant as Lucien de Rubempré sporting his new getup at the Tuileries and ogling himself in the eyes of passersby. What's happened to you? Doesn't your mom buy your clothes at Manby's anymore? (crumpled-ball question flicked by an expert finger to her table corner behind the Lagarde and Michard). NO HONEY IT COMES FROM PREBAC'S MY COUSIN'S TAKING ME TO A PARTY THIS AFTERNOON IN A CELLAR WITH LITTLE BLUE LIGHTS (ball answer exactly between the leaves of my binder). The little shit. A party with Blue Lights. Never would my folks have bought me a black T-shirt, the color of vice and fatality, and a skirt split in front and tight on the hips, to go down to some cellar where there'd be nothing but people flirting like mad with loud, languorous slow dances playing in the background. To think that that bitch had been sitting on her secret until the last minute, that must have been getting her wet for a whole month, this party business, and what about her girlfriends, tough out of luck. A Krunch Bar was good enough for us. Naval battles. Monopoly. Obviously she was almost four-teen and I thirteen. Between the two, the sound barrier. A spatial virginity. Suddenly in my rage I nabbed the Krunch Bar on its second round and broke off several squares at once and I began to chomp furiously, in the grips of a genuine compensatory bulimia, which sparked such a racket of protest that Mme. Roustignac in the middle of drawing a polder in cross section spun around and roared with the finger of justice pointing at the next-to-the-last row: GET OUT! SCHMAUZ, HIRSCH, TRISTAN, LARBAUD, UHLMANN AND BENSOUSSAN, OUT! Leave the room, head straight for study hall and don't forget to stop at the Disciplinarian's office beforehand. Always the saaaame ones, she croaked, watching our more or less high-spirited procession march past. They sleep, they snore, they stick their fingers in their noses, they pick their teeth, they chew, any day now they'll be painting their toenails right in class.

And while the North Sea was covering miles of polders under a genuine tidal wave, we rushed to Cloclo's.

Without Cloclo's existence, life would have been impos-sible given the time we spent at the clinic or in study hall, either after getting actually thrown out or as a precautionary measure. Cloclo was twenty-three and a militant in the Communist Party, having landed a job as a student aide in a lycée to earn enough money to get by and be able to conduct her political activities part-time and eventually do some recruiting. I met her one day on the Faubourg Poissonière in front of the *Humanité* office from where she led me off for something to drink in an attempt to indoctrinate me and, no doubt believing she had made me into a disciple, got into the habit of greeting me when our paths crossed in the corridors with a resounding, "Hello, comrade!" somewhat compromising, given that in those days the Lamartine lycée was far from being a bastion of the left. So I could thank Karl Marx for all the excuse notes I needed and the absences erased from the rollbooks; Karl Marx and Cloclo protected the life I led off the beaten track and it was well worth spending a few hours at the corner café with one ear attuned to the passages from *Das Kapital* that Cloclo recited to us by heart with the faith and blind proselytism of God's Holy Fools.

II

The Age of Violence

"All true freedom is black and inevitably comes to be one and the same as sexual freedom which is also black, without anyone clearly knowing why."

Antonin Artaud,
le Théâtre et son double

The Second Metamorphosis

In blood are we born. I came into the world a second time the day when, while washing, I saw a red stain on my sheet. It was in Cabourg, the night before Easter.

Much later, reading books and listening to my girlfriends' confidences, I learned that for many of them the arrival of the first period had been a disaster, a calamity, a shame, a revolting mess, the punishment for original sin, etc. An in-escapable taboo, lasting for five whole days, afflicted the unfortunate girls who made sauces turn, pricked themselves upon touching a needle, and forced any and everything male in their surroundings to flee, horrified by the odor. Plague-stricken, soiled, and *twelve times impure,* relegated to the accursed hut away from the tribe, witches, crushed under the weight of an age-old fatality, the "indisposed" girls punctually turned up at the clinic every twenty-five or twenty-six days, wrapped up in elastic girdles, lashed with diaper pins, a napkin as thick as a bolster between their legs, with rings under their eyes and a guilty look, and I also, a faithful visitor to this haven of peace claiming certain disorders of the gallbladder related to the hour math class was rostered, there I was completely flat, smooth as a palm from top to bottom, I envied those stupid gooses all caught up in their femininity, those monsters of resignation with their sick calf heads, I would have gladly given a good pound of my flesh for somebody to stretch me out as they were on a couch, and stick a moist towel on my forehead and have me chew a cube of sugar dipped in mint spirits.

So I had at last officially emerged from my childhood prison. Or at least, I no longer felt alone behind the bars; there was also Polline and the other girls in the class. Oh the goddamn passive waiting. But I needed proof, a bit of blood as an initiation, to have my right to a solar existence recognized. When I discovered that honest-to-goodness stain on my bed, I thought I would burst with happiness. I sat on the blanket and sank into a contemplation of the tiny red trace, seeking to interpret its meaning. It was an exotic butterfly, or two winged dragons face-to-face. I would like her to have lips as red as blood and skin as white as snow, said the queen thinking of the little girl she wished for—she pricked herself and a scarlet drop beaded on her wounded finger. Blood and snow. The strange and terrible nobility of this liquid that is neither seen nor heard nor smelled and yet circulates from the roots of the hair to the tips of the toes. All it takes is a little accident to shatter this false peace, break the body's illusive silence—a tiny little accident, and you find yourself before this raw, scarlet, imperial reality: blood, the color of life and of shameless, violent revolution. Nineteenth-century girls were taught that their veins ran with barley water and cabbage juice, so when it started to piss all they had to do was to flee the truth, to refuse it: to faint. I who had always liked the hot, insipid taste of my blood, who sucked myself, licked myself, vampirized myself as soon as a breach opened up, I would really have loved to experience the taste of the kind flowing at the bottom of my belly, but the stain dried and, as it gradually darkened, took on the sumptuous hue of Baccarat roses.

Perhaps I had already stepped to the other side of the looking glass, since inside I no longer recognized the appearance of things. Who was this scrawny girl in the white nightgown, in the middle of her open thighs a trickle of red liquor the color of church wine? And those eyes. Were those eyes mine, barbwired with lashes vibrating like a paramecium's, those eyes as opaque as hard stones, those agate eyes that had just pierced the fog and had begun to see? Were those pointy shoulders mine, the clavicles as straight as two ivory rulers pushing to the surface of the skin, that barest hint of breasts, that belly of a kid who suffers from air in the stomach and eats too much cake? And down there, the unknown. Two furrows, two small streams of blood that were blue, forked, branching, hidden in the hollow of the crotch, in the place where the skin is white, creamy, and sickly due to its softness, and farther down, genitals—a nail scratch, which hadn't much to do with the whole business. It was most especially at stomach level that the upheaval was located. A scratched stomach and guts thanked me for their wet heavy wound, the Devil's claw, fire and flood, a prickling burn and a reflection floating with splattered moons. And what if I was dreaming? What if I had cut myself on some glass? If somebody had slashed my pussy with shards in order to punish me? For what? Well, you've always done something wrong, ever since that little number with the apple. I touched the slit and drew away my vermilion-colored finger. No, no bits of glass. It's funny, I am as hollow as a tree trunk, I thought. Hollow as those round billboard columns in the streets. And I felt my legs go wobbly as if I had just been plopped in front of the Holy Grail; I felt like splattering myself with fresh blood, filling up the bidet with it and sticking in my feet, doing a lipstick drawing on the mirrors of enormous scarlet genitals, open, pulpy, and moistened like lips and elongated like squash; from my belly came rushing down all the rivers of the earth, the waters of the Ganges had its source at the roots of my

life and flowed from my mystical wound; all around me I felt
the phosphorescence and the wet shimmer of Salammbô's
zaïmph, all around my head floated a little of the diffuse
bluish glow stolen from the moon's corona, queen of
moisture, the ever-changing sticky uterine cavern of night.
In my belly, an earthquakened crust, sea trenches opened
up, Atlantic ridges, wounds of gleaming coral, a whole
Labrador which flowed toward the barely open estuary of
my sex where palpitated lichens and starry foam caressed
by the primordial tide, the tide that eats away at chalk cliffs,
the wine-colored tide that had also made me crumble away,
had invaded me, infested me, flooded me, gobbled me up by
the root and picked me clean down to the level of a
peneplain only to leave me there, crucified, stretched out
on the ground with open thighs licked by a luminous ruby-
colored foam.

*

On the same day, passing in front of the Casino, I barely had
time to step back a few feet to avoid these maniacs on
motorbikes who were detouring around the square with a
horrible roaring sound. Black jackets, I thought, real ones,
made out of studded leather, and Levis, pointy boots and
bicycle chains. Goddamn it, what a great time they must be
having, and I stood there fascinated, madly jealous of the
girls clinging like insects to these big guys all in black,
bound to them by sheer speed like those who love to set
their heads spinning plastered by centrifugal force against
the turning wall of the big amusement rides at fairs. They
slowed down, stopped in front of the Casino movie house,
and jumped down from their extraterrestrial tanks turned

back into a magnificent magma of mechanical guts. Rrrroh guys, I whispered in my corner. That one over there with the tiger on his back.

They had gone in to see the movie; *Warlock,* with Henry Fonda, was playing. I handed over my six francs and got a ticket. No problem spotting them in the darkness; they were blocking the whole bottom of the screen with their feet up on the seats of the row in front. The lights came on partially; Jean Mineur sent his knife flying right at the target, and the usherette loudly sang out: Eskimo pops, gumdrops, caramels, Nuts Bars! in her stewardess voice. A Nuts, please, I whispered as low as possible, not to call any attention to myself. What do you want? the usherette barked. A Nuts! I repeated in a voice that was more and more faint. A what? she bellowed, leaning forward and training the beam of her flashlight upon me, at which point the whole row turned around all at once and a tomb-like silence buried the room. The young lady would like a Nuts Bar, one of the boys murmured with pouting lips. You're a little deaf, granny. SO NUTS BARS FOR EVERYBODY! he roared and THEY'RE ON US. How much do we owe you, my tropical bird? Including the little girl's. Okay. Here. Take it, he told me holding out the bar wrapped in its yellow paper. Then, seeing me tear the Nuts Bar out of its wrapping with a trembling hand, he began to hum: "Take a look at her, so cute, can you tell me where she lives ah-ah," and the whole gang echoed it in chorus, clapping their hands while the terrified usherette fled with her supply of gumdrop-caramel candy. You're a little young but in a few years you'll be a big hit, sweetheart, the philanthropist added—a real big hit. Hey the movie. *Zee mouvee.* It started. *Bye-bye baby.* And he sank down into his seat so far that all I could see of him was a hairy mop and the points of cowboy boots.

Following the movie was out of the question anymore. I

took a very precise bite out of my Nuts Bar, panic-stricken at
the thought that my admirer could turn around again to
speak to me and praying that he would, my head ringing,
closing my eyes to savor all the better the moment and the
fresh outer coating of blessed chocolate which crinkled
against my taste buds, without a thought for the wild chases,
the overturned stagecoaches and the mined train tracks
exploding up there, in this Western that paled when compared to reality. Before the end of the movie, I slipped out to
contemplate my still intact happiness, as deep as the secret
fissure which, while opening, grazed my belly like a lash
made of rose thorns.

*

Thus reality, so impossible to grab hold of for so long,
suddenly leaped right into my face. Until then, I saw all of
creation as a scattered puzzle, an imaginary country that
was both delightful and full of despair where the violence of
disappointed dreams warped cathedral spires into a pyre
licking as high as the heavens, but the garden of Oneiroland
was also a place of torture; all I stole from the trees were
topaz pears impossible to bite into, the peppercorns on
my steak metamorphosing into brilliants, an incense boat
stolen at once by an eagle that carried them off to his lair in
the Valley of the Diamonds; I for one would have preferred
eating a plain, decent Pear Williams and a simple little
undercut, real horseflesh; the only problem was that truth
skidded out of control every single time in such a head-
spinning way that I also let myself be speeded off in the
eagle's talons, mountain passes higher than the Hindu
Kush swept under me, and shadowy valleys at the bottom

of which black birds stood watch over their brood of jewels, and while I hovered above the Temple of Ekni, Lord of the Abyss, dangling from the claws of my bird of prey and carried along in the dives and loop-the-loops in the void, my mother said: So Lydie is NEVER going to clean her plate.

And suddenly the skidding came to a halt, Scheherazade's eagles had transported me into another kingdom and set me delicately down on the ground in a real landscape—you could knock, punch, the mountains weren't made out of cardboard anymore nor was the water a mirage, there it was, divine, goddamned reality, even more astonishing than the feverish and exhausted nightmare of my schizophrenic childhood, a dream that always left me swindled and stunned with solitude.

The veil had been torn open upon the spells of the real world. The least LIVING things made me go wild. In Bagatelle, I spent hours looking at flowers, especially pansies, small rustic garnet muffles stabbed with pale yellow, and Notre-Dame appeared to me in all its glory like a huge dinosaur skeleton flanked with crutches, a ship moored on the Seine like the Empress Tseu-hi's marble boat on the lake of the Summer Palace, surrounded by a clear, tremulous light like the kind bathing Mont-Blanc, Mont-Saint-Michel and other wonders of the world that I had never thought to see.

Strolling from Place Pigalle to Montholon Square, I walked through the heart of a Europe concentrated in the ninth arrondissement, hiding treasures that I had taken thirteen years to discover, masterpieces on display within hand's reach, provocative, innocent, grinning, cruel, beaming, indecent, far more dazzling than those dozing in museums —all the Chardins in the world were not worth spit next to these stalls of fruits and vegetables in the street market, the dry stiff bouquets of the cabbages, the winey red of the beets, the fluffy-fleshy pink of the peaches, the jelly-like shimmer of the bristle-tail fish, and the obscene color of the tripe revealed by the raw light of the small electric bulbs that gave an indescribably tragic look to the faded red of the large beef carcasses hanging from the hooks—all of France was swarming on the rue des Martyrs at seven in the evening, wandering between mountains of blood sausage and camemberts, trampling the crumpled endive leaves, wallowing in a (feel-good) blessed medieval filth, a touching twilight muck steeped in a gypsum brightness, heading down from the satanic heights of Pigalle, baguette under arm, as far as the church of Notre-Dame-de-Lorette in the evening grazed by shadows that a poor springtime tinted the sad blue of hydrangea petals.

Before, ethereal ectoplasm that I was—ectoplasm, what am I saying, decalcomania, placental scraping—I would have shuddered with disgust before all this food, this tide of fatty bacon and veal marengo, the sight alone of which today filled in the enormous hole opening up in the place where my stomach was, the atmosphere alone of this big street market, this belly, this paunch fed me through the nostrils, and the rich odor of cockerels revolving on their spits made my mouth water like the dog of good old Pavlov, all the more if it was the fragrance of days off from school, the gargantuan mouth-watering mystical aroma of Sundays, days of chicken and staying in bed all morning.

At the butcher's, I always met the same ones in line, the people who used to scare me so stiff at one time that I would let any of that spineless bunch filch my place in line without making a peep; I now gazed at these housewives from the top of my tiny ogress's waist, women rummaging in their pocketbooks with a haggard, resigned look, announcing for all the world to hear the development of their daughter's ovarian cyst or of the tapeworm in their cat's bowels, and then they were off with their package in hand, purged and absolved of a large part of their woes—once again that's all it was, the seven circles of Hell, the Judges, the Others, this pitiful column of ladies all in a row, this conglomeration of mothers exactly the same as all those I didn't know. Turks, Bashkirs, Kirghiz and Tamils, fertile receptacles, walking ovulation machines, intermediary links between two generations who had stood, were standing, and will stand around in front of the butcher's to buy the ration of proteins that will add an extra day to their lives, thanks to which the Wheel of the Law will turn once more so that the cycle of Karmas will be perpetuated, karmanations and reinkarmanations, while the Jackal God Anubis disguised as a butcher, roly-poly, ruddy, wrapped in an apron spotted with a star of blood, worked upon his meat as if it were a dress, with supple movements, cutting the fat from the lean or barding with lard, wrapping with string vertically, horizontally and tossing the future veal roast on the scale of the ages, like the heart of the dead upon the scale of truth, with a sidelong glance scrutinizing the wavering needle of destiny that decided if souls should be thrown to the lions with crocodile maws or ceremoniously ushered before the tribunal of Black Osiris.

*

At the same time, my relationship with my mother underwent a radical transformation and I could no longer figure out the psychological reactions of this person who had always demonstrated a subtle moderation, changed now into a Mommy-Creature, sporadically possessed by a chthonian spirit that shook her from head to toes, made her shriek, drool, foam at the mouth, writhe about on the ground, and lunge at me with the full intention of ploughing her nails into my face, uttering incomprehensible words while vomiting up a flow of boiling lava: if the objects in the room didn't start waltzing around by themselves, Mommy took care of that, which forced me to quickly run and hide under the desk, the table, or the nearest shelter the very second when, by imperceptible signs, a light sweat, a shrinking of the pupils, a swelling of the thyroid, a quivering of the lower then of the upper limbs, a pinching-in of the lips or cheeks, the spirits manifested their presence, spirits who suck up flesh from inside and make the faces of the possessed look skeletal the way they will only after they've died. Then Echou, Ochala, Iansen or any of the other orishas that came from Brazil by way of the African jungle unleashed its fury in the human form of its liking, as it so happens here, my mother, sometimes even shifting its shape to an animal's, and while she whinnied and kicked out her hooves, roared like a lioness, growled like Bagheera from the heart of the Nepalese Terai, I wondered through what chink the incubus could have stolen in. Nights when the moon was full, Ahriman himself from the high Iranian plateaus came tumbling down inside Mother like Santa Claus through a chimney, and I can't say I was crazy about that, because she displayed all the symptoms of Saint Vitus's dance, or was it Tjalong Arang the black widow of Bali speaking through her mouth—I wouldn't have blinked an eye if I had been told that at these times she shoved a broom up her thingy so she could fly like the wind and meet up with the other witches of the sabbath on the slopes of Javanese volcanoes. Fortunately, once the demon's voice gave out, it disappeared, leaving Mother in a state of utter exhaustion, once again resembling the charming creature I had always known, but more or less unable to speak.

The weirdest thing was that all it took to summon Ahriman and gang was me leaving out a pair of socks on a bed, or coming home a half hour after I was supposed to or calling up Polline from under the desk where I holed up so I wouldn't be disturbed, trifles that were so out of proportion to the terrifying cyclone they unleashed. At those times if Mom had had her hands on a bazooka, torpedo boats, Mirages, tanks, cannons, a Beretta, or a flamethrower, I'm sure I would have known about it, but thankfully she only had a few rockets at her disposal, so all I needed to do was duck. In fact, Polline's mother also displayed symptoms, but somewhat attenuated, because of her moody personality and a rather marked indifference toward her offspring. Neither Polline nor myself tried to figure out what was really behind all these goings-on, nor even to challenge the right of absolute control our mothers had over us—after all, we might have made an effort to get rid of the spirits with a few rounds of therapy sessions, some holy water or an exorcism, or sacrificing chickens' feet cut off at St. Peter's, or lighting candles in Notre-Dame-de-Lorette; what I mean is made an effort to get to the bottom of their hang-ups and reopen the lines of communication between us and them, but no way; to be honest with you, that would have shaken up the laziness which had become a habit with us, that huge languorous, affectionate, and epicurean idleness which winds itself around you from the beginning of your adolescent years like a voluptuous python, a snug and sensual sluggishness that goes hand in hand with a complete intellectual apathy, rusting up the mechanism that will only get going again far in the future, because back then all our energy was tied up on the level of cellular exchange with nothing left over for anything else; we were still growing up, we had pimples on our foreheads, and in out guts, geologic upheavals; we were adolescing full steam ahead, we were coming into our full-belly period, sticky, spongy, fluffy with grains of pollen while behind us we left a trail of sparkling spores like a comet's tail. So between this miracle of narcissistic bullshit—our fourteen years and our mothers' dispositions—stood a wall. No matter how many sleepless nights they spent, they could not crack our secret Swahili, not even by throwing our tubes of mascara in the trash or opening our mail and turning it into toilet paper while threatening to shut us away in a cage like the late La Ballue; all these spiteful schemes merely reinforced the high opinion Polline and I had about our philosophy of life, based on the theory of Apocalyptic Desire, which could crystallize around a pair of shoes, or going to the movies, or any dream at all that had to be acted on right away before it went up in smoke. We were splitting at the seams with our End-of-Worlditis, swollen up like some fat cloud stalled over the plain of Orissa; while waiting for the power to burst upon the world in disastrous funnels of rain, we let loose any way we could, we cooked up stories, we stole false eyelashes from perfume counters, we trafficked in birth-control pills—and most of all we HATED, absolutely hated, the truth.

If you emptied out on a table the bag of tricks of a teenager, a "teenie" as Thieuloy calls them, you'd find all jumbled up in a heap: crumpled movie tickets, Pharoah lipstick ripped off from a department store, fake love letters sent to ourselves, a few crumbs of the tobacco that fell out of the Kents we smoked back then, our calendars nicknamed Cutie, and words committed to memory: "If you want to be happy, be it," a saying by Sacha Guitry we used as an epigraph because of its inspired, commanding simplicity. Then, the secret code. Namely: flirting = going to the Louvre, kissing = Greek Antiquities Room, to be in the lap of = Flemish Painting, to go to the movies with = Egyptian Room, a party = have a light snack, drugstore = Napoleon's

Tomb. Let me point out that we had never even been there, nor kissed a guy, but around school all we heard were the tales of Fisher's and Papazian's epic adventures, the two of them rounding at full speed the cape of fourteen-and-a-half, who scoured the Champs Elysées from top to bottom, meaning from the one and only Drugstore to the Renault Pub where they met up with their gang of friends on Thursday afternoons, and Saturdays and Sundays, and were led off to surprise parties. I'd have given my blouse to be in on that. What am I saying? My brand-new Bally shoes—the same as Schmauz's—and even my panties. Only thing, NEVER once would Fisher or Papazian have brought us along, the bitches; they kept that good deal for themselves and no way would they give any of their girlfriends a break.

*

So dreams were no longer some kind of sickly, psychic stomachache, but had changed into a surrealist game, exquisite and self-infatuated, whose rules we knew backwards and forwards. The witches had vanished, the Carthusian Cat meowed instead of talked, and the sky prison, where Vivien had shut me up for my whole childhood like the wizard Merlin, had evaporated like the dew marks of a fairy's breath. I was no longer possessed by uncontrollable images, I no longer fled into fiction so I could escape the panic life filled me with; I made things up the way I breathed, for no reason but the sheer joy of it.

In the past I hugged walls as fragile as stiff frosting, stealing along on tiptoe between paper-thin carpets where the perspective lines blurred over each other toward a vanishing point located in some faraway antimatter, brushing up against a stage set that now all I needed to do was flick with one finger for it to come crumbling down, exposing the back side of the flat.

From now on, we decided to embark on our inner journeys as if we were tripping out on mescaline; we got stoned on almond glue and ether with our eyes wide open; we stuffed our faces with toast buttered with illusion knowing full well when to call it quits before we got sick to our stomachs, and when we changed sizes, growing as tall as the Kanchenjunga or as small as indivisible atomic particles, we knew that we would get back to our so-called normal dimensions any time we wanted, so we really went right at it, we went through the gateway of dreams, ducking to be sure not to bang our heads; we strode the royal path of the chimeras, we tickled the chins of the stone lions along the alley that led to the Ming tombs, we created new races of beings—the Purple People who reproduced exclusively by means of parthenogenesis; in this new-found Oneiroland any rational question was punished by paying a fine—for example, pinching Béchefigue in the fatty back of her arm until she screamed right in the middle of Latin class. Nights we dressed up like Judex or Fantomas and we cut loose burglarizing chic apartments. There were some amazing ones—for example, this villa in Saint-Cloud where we slipped in after breaking a windowpane with a cupping glass and a diamond-tipped razor, and what do we find but a hallway going on and on where this unbroken mass of shadows was being projected, wandering all over the walls like a slow mitosis of cells tinted blue with methylene, while in the bathroom the scale dial kept the time, and in the Louis Quinze living room, which looked like Mme. Méry-Guichard's, wine filled the cups instead of tea, and instead of woodwork along the walls there were stovepipes covered with real gold, and in the dining room painted mirrors stood in the place of paintings whose only trace was the empty frames left behind, and this brass doll, done up like a cardinal, was ensconced on a commode at the end of the hallway, and— LARBAUD TELL ME A LITTLE SOMETHING ABOUT ATALA'S DEATH . . .

Late Morning Delinquency

"The aim of life is to live, however bizarre and unilateral that may appear. The totality of life's meaning is life itself, the process of life—one must first love life, let oneself be completely submerged in it. . . ."

from the diary of the pupil Kostia Riabsteve, in Wilhelm Reich, *The Sexual Revolution*

The Gaumont Palace has been destroyed and the Drugstore has burned down. The Drugstore, the one and only, near the Arch d'Triumph. The gang is gone that used to come tearing down the Champs-Elysées pounding the macadam with their boots from Winston's. The movie houses have turned into five-headed hydra-like things and the newsstores, the Elyséestores, the thingamajigstores, proliferating, are nothing more than the cankers of superconsumption. Our dreams have been shattered and our magic years have been burned for witchcraft; the black flag of anarchy dangles pathetically like a scorched shred planted on a gigantic scoop of ice cream, a mountain of runny, heartbreaking sugar, a gob of whipped cream with almonds on top that they want to force those who are now fifteen to swallow, persuading them that this is how life really tastes, all soft, sweet, creamy, milky—as for me, I remember that at that age life tasted like rotgut, rubbing alcohol, pure absinthe, ginseng root, essence of heliotrope, red phosphor, raw opium, Jamaican pepper, a pinch of spices from the Molucca Islands that permanently scorched your mouth and guts forever.

We were all starving and sex-starved, as Henry Miller says, afflicted with a permanent hunger which drove us like beasts of prey upon everything that was proposed as appetizing, brilliant, garish, a turn-on, gobbling up 45s, color film, miles of road as if the human race were going to disappear right after us and we had to hurry up and take advantage of the sunshine before being eliminated from the planet as the dinosaurs had been, which now weren't much use to anybody. We knew that life was only good if you stayed hard and hungry, with your belly feeling a little empty, and that the best moment was *before,* when you feel free, vacant, at once stretched like a bow by desire and filled with the great vacuum of interstellar spaces. We shed our skins each season like boas, we died and were reborn every morning, we torched everything behind us like barbarians of the fifth century, feeling only one thing for certain: that all around us stretched the steppes of fatalism, of resignation, of last gasps, acrawl with dying larvae who had known all about ration coupons, had heard the whistling of the bombs above their heads and had wanted only one thing: to lead an existence hugging the ground, all doped up and draftproof, and lure us into their caves never to come out again into the open air, whereas we really had to fill our lungs to bursting before the explosion of the cosmic Bengal light, the unleashing of the last plague upon Egypt, the slow unfolding of the cobalt mushroom.

*

While waiting, the scale of the perceptible world had changed. I noticed this upheaval upon arriving in the Vendée at the beginning of July 1964. Pornic had shrunk. Yet the rue de la Source still climbed straight up; not one section of the wall of Gilles de Rais's castle had crumbled and high tide still covered the Gois with the speed of its horses of surf, but I was afflicted with adolescence, this pruritus, this eczema that was such a turn-on to scratch, and I was temporarily blind to everything that was not the pleasure principle; I had lost my sorcerer's wand and let go the reins of the fantastical ostriches carrying me on their backs along the Orinoco; I could no longer tell apart ultraviolet and infrared, I had become deaf to the murmur of the underground streams and I no longer heard in seashell horns the spluttering of the oceanic beer. In my enraged boredom I punched jellyfish in their stomachs, those violet-streaked windbags aquiver like seaweed puddings, I sent a few swift kicks flying at them unafraid of their sting, certain that instead of being fatal like Nessus's shirt, at the very most all it could give me was a pretty bad case of hives; I walked through Birochère like Gulliver in Lilliput, crushing under my soles the castles of childhood, ramparts of sand that the sea encrusted with seashell shards, porcelainized or brilliant like the specks of an *aventurine* before being leveled with big licks, pathetic fortresses that I had demystified like the salt pyramids of Noirmoutiers in the heart of which not the least mummy slept, no more than the seaweed blisters popped with my thumb were toads' eyes, nor the juice running between my palms, the piss of the Nereids.

And yet appearances had remained the same. July Fourteenth, we still made our lantern-light procession on the corniche toward Gourmalon, a medieval name whose echo did not even disturb the sleep of the knights in the nave of Artus any longer, and when the Eole took us out on the open ocean for the Blessing of the Water with the gym teacher and the priest throwing wreaths into the waves and releasing pigeons, I no longer hoped to be taken all the way to the Cyclades. Local festivities threw me into fits of rage; I categorically refused to dress up as a shepherdess or in seer-sucker hollyhock in order to make the rounds on a chair and see myself awarded twelfth-place costume prize, and nothing was more of a pain in the ass than going for tea with the ladies from the Château de la Birochère, whose cele-brated Portcullis Park and path of dwarf palms at one time gave me the impression of passing into the fourth dimension. The only thing escaping this shipwreck was the Saint-Michel galettes that came with tea (made in Saint-Michel-Chef-Chef since 1905) which simultaneously crunched and melted under my teeth and whose shortbread taste, flavored with rum, reawakened the memory of my escapades with the neighbor's boy, as confused as the recollection of a former life buried under strata of consciousness, as uncertain for me as the memory of having lived, so very long ago, the life of a priestess of Isis or a troubadour's at the court of the Capitouls in Provence.

*

In the month of September 1964, war was declared on the powers that be. A latent war, fought by ambush. Polline had just come down with being fifteen years old, the way you catch a cold; her life was a long series of delicious sneezes,

and I moved forward through my fourteenth year without my
parents noticing a thing, except maybe for my grandmother
who cast anxious glances in my direction, as if she had just
seen a succulent plant, a modest cactus for a Japanese
garden, abruptly start to rise as high as the ceiling. But all
this would be of merely anecdotal interest if a whole
generation hadn't started to grow up and flourish in the
sunshine in a state of total anarchy. A genuine jungle. It
branched out, became entangled, entwined every which
way. There was talk of scandal concerning Janson; the Black-
shirts gave way to the gold in the columns of newspapers.
For us, reality surpassed, as the expression goes, fiction. The
gods tumbled from Hymettus with a few specks of ambrosia
at the corners of their mouths and removed their sandals
made of wind before entering the Drugstore; no matter they
were wearing leather jackets and jeans, you could tell them
by their hyacinth curls and their kisses that left a heavenly
taste of honey on your lips.

We needed some breathing room. To blow everything
sky-high. To liquidate parents, royal pains in the ass before
Eternity, without taking the time to dwell on their psychological problems, just taking care to keep them outside of
our secrets by lying to them to our hearts' content, from
morning to night, without ever letting down our guard,
because instead of opposing them with a wall of silence
they had to be duped, duped the whole time; not for one
second could we stop our routines, for the consequence of
the least mistake would have been quite serious. A whole
mob of kids bursting their eardrums at the Golf Drouot,
swiping shetland sweaters at Renoma's, ravaging the apartments of the Avenue Foch, yanking up carpets, tossing TV
sets out of windows, trafficking in alcohol and contracep-
tives, taking a drag on their first joints at the Relais de
Chaillot in '64 before the newspapers had devoted a single

line to the subject believed to be dead and buried since Thomas de Quincey's time, came on to guys by the dozens, hell, what else, in short not giving one holy shit about all the moral taboos that formed the backbone of the preceding generation, all of which risked throwing sand into the gears of the great machine. So we led two parallel lives, at home and Outside, where the border lines of our kingdoms had in a flash shrunk considerably.

Until then, we crouched in our holes like frightened mice, our mouths watering at the dangers of the forest. I for one would have loved to extend the limits of my fiefdom as far as the Great Wall of China but, while waiting, I paced in circles in the sacred enclosure, the territory of childhood, the ninth arrondissement, between rue Mauberge, the Folies-Bergères, the kosher-products shop of Papazian's parents, rue Pigalle and Bensoussan's cellar with a view of the show at Chez Moune, Montholon Square and its billboard column, rue de la Chaussée d'Antin where Marguerite Gauthier's ghost was still wandering, the pastry shop that only existed for winter evenings when it gets dark at five o'clock, its fragrance of warm butter, the light of its pink neon letters, the heavy, acrid hot chocolate into which we dipped the points of our croissants, and its walls decorated with a stucco frieze of the four seasons in a vaguely Stainlesque style, the Dauphin movie house where I had seen one of my first movies during my grandfather's days, a story about a dam blown up on the Durance River—what had I left from my grandfather, only and especially the famous volume of the *Iliad* and the *Odyssey* in the Pléiade collection for which I had conceived ever since a mystical veneration, what a truly inspired present destined to determine my career, but Grandpop was asleep without knowing this— where was I? oh yes, in the passage named Verdeau, leading to Polline's, the Faubourg-Montmartre and the spells of the

Maghreb, the scummiest place in the world according to
Miller, where often there were knife fights between
Hungarians and Algerians at night, between Aron Son of
Tunis's shop, the Zazaou Brothers', and the reassuring
candy-store front, Something For Mother, founded in 1761,
in which you could even find Catalan torrone and pine nuts.

*

Fourteen years old. High-wire act across a silk cord, while
below, acting as a net, was the boarding school, the prison,
the cage, no less. We bootlegged, we cut ourselves off from
society, wild, hanging out, delinquent, grandchildren of the
century—sure, but which century? was it the end of the
Middle Ages or the eighteenth, no that sort of decadence
was subtle and poisonous like a pamphlet, filthy as the
private suppers of the Regency, whereas ours exploded
with an ingenuous health that resembled rage, a contagious
disease and a cannibal happiness, we had never left France
but, already, already we felt at home everywhere, *like kings,
streetwalkers and thieves.*

 We were probably involved in politics the way M. Jourdain
was in speaking his prose; that is, unawares we took up the
battle against a whining, constipated, arthritic society—we
didn't give a damn about this stockpile of canned food; all
we knew was that we didn't feel like climbing it. We suspected the existence of the system rather like a vague threat
weighing upon us, but the thought had not yet occurred to
us that we could escape any other way than by slipping
across, taking cover. The personification of the Machine
was our parents, come from another planet, unless we were
the ones whom they regarded as a race of mutants. In short,

the old scenery was crumbling, there were no more explosions on the mined landing beaches but somewhere else, very far away, heading toward Vietnam, and thousands of young rovers had already left the States and the northern countries to follow the passage to India, but back home in '64 people snored away with clenched fists.

*

Unfortunately, in our entourage there were neither kings, nor whores, nor thieves, only desperately grayish people, the color of walls and crushed bugs, street people who hid pathetic little mysteries behind their raised overcoat collars, faces eroded by routine, like the concierge Nénette; the widow Mme. Caron and her five stuffed cats; the General and his orderly who threw the Saint-Quentin street market into an uproar when he strolled through there in the morning dressed as a woman with diamond earrings; Mme. Minard the butcher, a classic hysteric; Mme. Trousset, a genuine mountain, an hydropic giantess who had attended the same religious boarding school as my grandmother and who had been driven by financial setbacks to become a cleaning lady; Pilar, the fine, decent Spanish woman who had smothered her husband by shutting him in the bathroom after having rigged the water heater during the days when she served at an Italian countess's—and the lycée teachers, Mlle. Lipman, who skipped the passages of Latin translation as soon as they dealt with Antony and Cleopatra; Mme. Méry-Guichard or the Revolution; Mlle. Roustignac, the geography teacher who had developed a confused affection for me; finally the gang—Schmauz, Hirsch, Papazian, Uhlmann and Bensoussan—I pass over Polline, precious particle of myself.

Delinquency, psychologists say, generally begins by playing hooky. Cutting classes turned into a habit, which cost us
an arm and a leg—two francs' worth of apple turnovers for
Bensoussan every time. We fully realized that, despite
Cloclo's good intentions, the tardies and zeros accumulating
like lava in the chimney of a volcano would all end up by
erupting one day, but for the moment we preferred not to
think about it and to lock ourselves up in our citadel of
secrets. We ran off from morning to night, if only to walk
through Paris, a praying-mantis city with diamond tentacles,
to follow along the string of streets strewing the ramparts of
Time and to spell out the neon signs belting the sooty walls,
whose blinking Morse code we deciphered; we painted our
faces with gall, rust and coal in Paris-Babylon, whore with
spread thighs daubed with mercury; we watched the
phosphorescent night brighten its iron light behind the
black trees of the Bois de Boulogne and on the Seine the
shimmer of the secret fire smoldering in the heart of pearls;
we pushed our palets onto the magic mandala of the arrondissements, we plunged into the heart of this hollow planet
riddled with catacombs, sewers, and asphalt corridors where
mad trains hurtled along; each square yard of sidewalk
possessed its adventure, dawn rose with the color of crime
at the Impasse des Brouillards and the Quai de Javel, golden
ectoplasms stretched their legs around the Cour Carrée,
rapiers clinked on rue Guisarde, the flash of a switchblade
pierced the darkness on rue Orfila, above the Quai de
l'Horloge floated a dais riddled with stars, a cut hand pissed
blood on rue Lacenaire, excuse me Lacordaire, Quai des
Deux-Berges, the hair of the drowned drifted between two
currents like the spongy tentacles of sea anemones, it
smelled of incense and hallelujahs in the direction of the
city of Heliopolis, and on the stage of the Rex intermittent

fountains came to life while on the ceiling died the electric galleries of a fake Moroccan sky under which the cupolas of Islam, white as clouds, were guarded by the Delphic Auriga erect in her stucco alcove. You would have needed a whole life to explore the grand Snakes and Ladders game of these surrealist streets, porcelainized like the rue de la Chine, glacial like the Impasse du Labrador or rue Froidevaux, with blood clotted around a calf's head on a butcher-shop's marble slab, cosmic whorey streets like rue de la Lune, streets as fluid as sea currents, as torrid as the Oyo Shivo or polar like the Kouro Shivo, yellow and blue like the great rivers of Asia.

And winter. Never was Paris more regal than that particular winter when it snowed and snowed. The Tuileries basins were set trembling with a shuddering as pale as ivory, the evening sky all violet-cracked over Place Vendôme; we jumped across the gutters solidified into sugar candy, and we brought down the parapets of slush the way we broke the frosting of tender, pasty, glazed chestnuts with one bite, the snow melted on our tongues in a cold vanilla powder, as anesthetizing as sherbet, that hussy Paris glittered with slate-gray sapphires, rough diamonds and aquamarines like the palaces of the ancient kings of Siam, and the champagne we drank on the sly from tooth cups had the fruity taste of a tide of pink stars.

*

As for kings, fat chance we had of meeting any in the immediate future. But whores, now they were just around the corner. Whores exercised an absolute fascination upon Polline, who had gotten expelled from elementary school for having answered the teacher's indiscreet question about her future, saying that she would marry a doddering old man loaded with dough and that she wouldn't lift a goddamned finger, using other words, but it came down to the same thing: at which point the teacher rose to her feet, drained of color and wailed: MADEMOISELLE LARBAUD YOU'LL END UP WALKING THE STREETS, a prediction Polline took quite literally as the disguised sign of a predestination of sorts.

However, one January day, upon opening the door to her father's clients in place of the flu-stricken maid, Polline fell in love with a vaginitis with trichomoniasis. Vaginitis, very elegant in a pink rabbit-fur coat, looked like she was only wearing little lace panties and disinfected her pussy with essence of marjoram—impossible to suspect that within there was what I imagined as the secret breeding of a colony of termites, which according to Polline showed themselves to be particularly tough in fashionable people.

Hughette, gifted in all domains, after having left her parents and five sisters in Marseilles, had hopped the express up to Paris, where she had dug up a string of jobs, among others dog groomer, park chair attendant, go-go girl in a suburban nightclub, candy salesgirl in a self-service restaurant (my dream), and cashier in a porno movie house where she sat enthroned behind a ticket window fitted out in an enormous pink plaster phallus; then at the age of twenty-two had turned towards the profession of prostitution, wondering why in hell she hadn't done so sooner. This *why* had been discovered with the help of Abel, ex-philosophy teacher, poet and pederast, who shared his apartment on rue Richer and acted as her tutor, psychiatrist, all-around maid and cook. *Why?* because she had been given, plain and simply, a guilt complex by her parents and the priests at whose schools she had spent a rather short stay before running away for the first time when she was twelve. But now she turned her tricks with a perfectly clear conscience, in elegant neighborhoods, nowhere but the eighth and the sixteenth arrondissements, and she had her johns come to her place, with Abel passing as her pimp, which avoided any trouble whenever she encroached on the private hunting grounds of her girlfriends.

We listened to Hughette for hours on end, flopped on the sofa in her fortune-teller's hovel, or so as not to disturb Abel who was writing poems, in front of a glass of grenadine-flavored milk in the Tabac des Folies where a parade of dancing girls came to dope themselves up with a cup of coffee before sticking their feathers back on their fannies and squeezing into their belly buttons a ruby I imagined to be as big as the third eye.

The story of H. was something we soon knew by heart—the fabulous fairy-tale life of a whore. Sometimes she must have padded things a little but we were duped all the same, not so much by the luxury hotels, the caviar, and the sports cars as by the innate sense of organization which had driven her to make a selection of pedigree johns, among others the king of combat uniforms who came to see her once a week from Annecy and whose generosity alone might have been adequate to both her own and Abel's needs—but no, she had the profession in her blood, and just to keep from getting rusty she continued to get laid by small-time accountants, retirees, and darkies. Thanks to fucking guys who were all so different from each other, Hughette wound up acquiring a panoramic view of all of creation and really had what it took to write a history of mankind beginning with the Neanderthals, helped by the man to whom she owed all her education, Abel, the philosopher who had made the journey to the end of his night, all splattered with Sartrean nausea, who had found in her a disciple capable of soaking up his knowledge like a blotter and of learning by heart the poems of Boris Vian, whom he had known personally very well long ago; Hughette used with the same natural flair the most fascinating slang and the most erotic terms, the kind you found before only in textbooks, and we were astonished to discover that under the layers of dead frozen letters smoldered the lava of Krakatoa and Mount Pelée; all you needed was to stir the embers a little for it to start roaring. Hughette swore like a plumber and a Senegalese infantryman rolled into one, and quoted Chateaubriand. Transfusing her with his gay science by perfusions, intravenous shots, and—when those didn't work—electroshock, Abel had metamorphosed her into a kind of bipartite siren, her lower half thrashing above the swamp, gleefully sending gobs of mud in every direction, and her upper bathing in the essential light of a Fra Angelico.

We learned a whole lot more on rue Richer than we ever did in the lycée. At least there we dealt with life in the flesh, waltzing through our heads in a kaleidoscopic whirlwind, jumbling the story of Gandhi and of the fascist T'sin Che Huang, who had burned all the books; of Akhenaton the madman of the sun; of Faust and Raskolnikov; the Dadaist movement; the Lettrist group and the great drift of surrealism; from every and any direction we snatched bits of Breton, Eluard, Tzara, Shakespeare and Tagore, the whole mess in a sumptuous cathouse of confusion. Abel also brought us to the Louvre, whose rooms of Italian paintings he knew by heart and told us in front of Caravaggio's canvases, where he never neglected to pay a brief visit, that the painter had taken as a model for the Virgin the cadaver of a prostitute fished out of the Tiber, and when we left the museum all drugged up on the colors, we saw a shred of iridescent silver trailing on the Seine, a pool of Veronese crystallize pictural matter, a verdigris as subtle as the silken garments split with shadows that the doges wore in the Venetian paintings as big as the movie screen in the Gaumont Palace.

Hughette and Abel sent us rolling like a ground swell into a whirlpool of knowledge; we received the full brunt of the total mass of information capable of being transmitted to human beings, but in a raw state, neither channeled nor oriented nor impoverished, and its infinitude plunged us into a stupor of sorts, horrified and enraptured. With Hughette as intermediary, we plunged into the collective recesses she explored with a tireless tenacity. She HAD to make it with two or three strangers every day, merely to approach them, sniff them, touch them, undress them, massage them, take their pulse, pull their legs and some francs out of their wallets, grill them until they spit out the gobs lodged in their throats, and let them go on their way emptied of all their substance, the gray and the white, on which she fed like a praying mantis after having sliced the top off her mate's head to imbibe the brain. At times, much to her despair, she ran smack into a wall of incommunicability which she tore her nails against, working her fingers until a breach of brightness opened up. Her favorite was Pinot, a small-time traveling salesman who got thrown out of all the nightclubs because of his shyness and chronic hay fever that made his relationship with other people impossible—she took him in her bed, the traveling salesman, she cradled him, teased him, sweet-talked him until he felt sorry for himself; he emptied his wallet and translated his despair into a long cosmic howl, sessions that generally ended in a series of terribly violent sneezes, after which Pinot, emptied of his miasmas and mucus, greatly relieved, went off to sell his boot trees.

*

I do free-lance work, Hughette would say. No way she would have some Tom, Dick or Harry on her back. One-hundred to three-hundred francs a pop, and sometimes it lasts as long as ten minutes. Don't get my job mixed up with what the ten-franc chiselers in the Bois de Boulogne do, or the dumb cows on rue Saint-Denis. It's a matter of class. Besides, I'm forced to blow lots of dough on my getups. Just so you know everything, I get off all by myself as soon as the guy puts his cock up in my belly. I couldn't fuck for nothing anymore. Got to have the motivation. If I'm paid a lot, it's because I'm worth it. Having a guy without a penny to show for it, now that's robbery. Look, I'm a reactionary. In any case, a few bills is all it takes for me to get going, then watch out, the Thailandese wagon, the little Javanese train, the Malagache cable car and the Cantonese spinning top— doesn't mean a thing to you kids, you'll catch on later. To turn a trick is what every woman dreams of deep down. If you had any idea how many respectable middle-class wives you come across in the hotels. And the atmosphere . . .

At which point she launched into her favorite flight of purple prose: the tale of her first trick; she was spinning in orbit and we would be going until eight at night. So Polline and I, using our magic powers, entered into the game, we put ourselves in her shoes and with Hughette interposing, we relived that unique moment, somewhat enriched with our personal reflections, so well that by the third go-round of the story we saw a multitude of Hughettes, of Pollines and Lydies undressing in front of multitudes of mirrors in an anonymous hotel room.

—The first time I got off for dough, Hughette would begin, it was to replace a friend who had scorched her willy by spreading on a double layer of gray ointment. Sure, mercury kills crabs, but it also gave her second-degree burns. In short, she was on unemployment. So she had put me onto something, four-hundred francs clear, an hour's work. She took a one-hundred franc commission on that, which was normal. It was supposedly a deal made in heaven, a Polish guy loaded with dough, fiftyish and distinguished, everything your heart could desire except for one slight fetish: little feet. A sucker, a licker, a toe-nibbler, that was M. Vladimir, known as Vlad. Getting my toes all spic and span for three-hundred francs, sure, I got into that just fine. Only thing was at fifteen I was still a virgin. I didn't like any of the neighborhood hoodlums enough to get screwed up against a trashcan on Saturday nights. Never ever would I have had the guts to admit that to my girlfriend, no way. So before ringing the bell, I'm so scared my stomach's spiraling in knots, and at the same time I feel like giggling because of the door plaque: Home Sweet Home. . . . In the end I chickened out, I tore down the steps, ran into a bar and downed a pastis. What with arranging everything, I hadn't had the time to do my toenails, my polish was flaking off and I was going to look like an absolute bummer in the maniac's eyes. Good thing I had some Cutex in my purse. So I went down to the toilets to put on an extra coat.

By this point of the story, I wasn't listening anymore, I was in those nightmarish toilets, slashed with white neon, four walls the nasturtium color of Hughette's nail polish, a thick red ooze, sticky and obscene like gushes of blood, the vibrations piercing my brain filled the whole glory hole and struck the wall with a crackling of scarlet sparks, the pastis burned my stomach; I must have arrived in Hell, things started to roast and sputter and smoke and scorch; if I didn't get out of this john, I was going to get grilled on my spit like a juicy milk-fed piglet. So I came back out into the fresh air, climbed to the Home Sweet Home, closed my eyes, took a deep breath and rang the bell. Time stood still until the door was opened and all I made out in the crack was the face of a nice old lady with blue-gray hair who looked more like an aunt from the provinces than the character Owl from *The Mysteries of Paris,* and she asked me if I had an appointment while giving me the once-over. Yes, with M. Vlad. Fine, you'll wait in the bedroom. He's never very late.

No doubt about it, the hell of depravity looked a whole lot like a boardinghouse. I was starting to find it all a real pain in the ass, like going to the dentist's, when she finally asked me a question that confirmed my hope that in one step I had finally crossed the barrier of prohibitions: Just how old are you exactly, honey? It's just that, you understand, with under-eighteen-year-olds I could get into trouble. . . . I'm nineteen, I boomed out, an answer which didn't seem to convince her because she added: Be especially careful not to run into anybody on the staircase.

Then she left me alone in the bedroom, and I savored the ultimate pleasure of finding myself, at last, in a state of absolute illegality. First off, I was fourteen; second, I was turning tricks; third, I was going to eradicate my virginity in one go with a Polish guy; fourth, I would be leaving the place with my pockets bulging with juicy bills, but that last part didn't get me off that much—well, just a little. Hughette was right—making love for money is an ideal magic relationship. Not to know a thing about the guy who is going to enter you, to put on your act for him, to say your name is Anais or Lola Lola, to fuck, good, pleasant or indifferent, only doing it counted, the essence of subversion, proof of my freedom—as for the dough, it was tainted, so if you didn't get hold of it by cheating it would lead you right into a sucker's trap, no way would I put it straight back into the system to buy myself a pair of shoes—absolutely not, I was going to stash it until I had enough to go all the way to Ceylon, Angkor, or South Yemen from where I'd never come back.

So there I was waiting for my Pole, behind my back sensing the irritated grumbling of two-thousand years of Judeo-Christian civilization, scared into such a blob of jelly that for reassurance's sake I had to try and persuade myself I was in this place by accident—after all I could have just as well been in a movie house or at home in a screaming match with my mother or playing pinball in the Tabac des Folies, instead of stewing in this bedroom, a masterpiece of kitsch, with its 1925 lamps and cream-colored fluted shades, with its artificial flowers, its pink-tinted ceiling mirrors—a genuine mirror chamber, as in the Musée Grévin—its corner sofa covered with a mauve satinet quilt with tassels on which sat enthroned, in the midst of its gold-threaded gauze skirts, a Spanish-style carnival doll. Still no Pole. So I wouldn't go completely off my rocker, I decided to put all my energy into my favorite concentration exercise: training my attention on a picture until I go into it and completely dissolve myself behind the wall of appearances, because all it takes is the tiniest mental stimulus to condense at once all the disorders of consciousness by eliminating the vortex of useless thoughts. So I picked a photo of the Temple of Karnak hanging above the bed and I set sail for Egypt; I was walking for a good while through the Valley of the Kings between lanes bordered with mute gods on my way to the necropolis of Seti the First, passing by processions of sacrifice bearers in shell robes who only showed me their slight profiles floating in a mournful light, with sacred ibises circling above my head while I was preparing to go down to the Nile in a felucca, when the door opened on the old lady and the Polack who uttered some incomprehensible hodge-podge of polite phrases whose aim was to play down the situation, followed by a "what do you want to drink," to which I responded a whiskey, despite the fact I disliked the stuff, it stinks like tiger piss—then I threw myself into the contemplation of my vermilion-painted toenails and stayed quiet, allowing the Polish guy all the time in the world to take a detailed inventory of my person. At that critical moment, I felt like I was stuck in an elevator rising to the fifty-ninth floor of a Manhattan skyscraper with a guy I didn't know, I would never know, that's how it is in those cases, the rub-a-dub-dub of magnetism that grates on your nerves, you're afraid your personal bubble's going to burst when it touches your neighbor's, it's a pain in the ass so you desperately focus on some arbitrary point in the air until the racking trip up comes to a stop, and you can at last recuperate the fragments of your crumbled aura.

He had a smell of wealth about him, of "wealfth" as Hughette said, who had her mouth crammed full as if she had just helped herself to a big gulp of caviar, a few particles of which were still sticking in her teeth, an odor seeping from under his camel-hair overcoat, his Italian leather briefcase and his gray hair scented with Hermès cologne, an intoxicating aroma that penetrated my whole body as if gold nuggets had been grafted into every pore of my skin. That kind of dough must have had the venerable patina of louis d'or minted with the effigies of kings. To what do I owe the pleasure, he said, of seeing you here in Hughette's place? His voice was rich too, mountains of coins loudly tinkling in the background, the treasure of the Nibelungen spread out right there in this small bedroom in Pigalle, enough to take a bath in pure gold—she's got ganglions, I said—I'm sorry to hear that, the Polack said, but so very pleased to meet you, you are a genuine Tanagra. And those tiny red nails, genuine petals. What's your shoe size? Five and a half, not any bigger, right? Show me your shoes. Well, the price is right but, as far as quality goes, I've seen better. I hope to have the pleasure of giving you some others. Exactly what do you want? —Uh, I say, then once I had gulped down the big shot of whiskey the old lady had just brought—bikers' shoes with eyelets. Obviously that wasn't exactly a professional choice but I wanted to be as with it as that lucky bastard Schmauz, I was dying with an Apocalyptic Desire for those bikers' shoes, the world's very existence depended on those soft leather shoes, BLACK, with square silver eyelets. And socks too, I added, real long ones. And socks, he repeated absently, his eyes fixed upon me. Then he started to laugh very softly, then more loudly, until he was crying, and he took me on his lap and said to me, fine, now I'm going to take off your clothes and I promise you can keep your socks on even in bed if it makes you happy—there he is thinking he's going to go in me like I was butter, he's got to find out the horrible truth, my taint, my real shame: that I'm still a virgin, blocked up, membraned; wow, I imagine that must be something awful, a layer harder than quartz, a diamond frontier, it would take a pneumatic drill to blast it apart. A virgin, dear sir, that's what I am. A Virgo? he said, the sly devil. Then. . . . Well, I didn't know anymore after that. My imagination ran dry. I had to believe Hughette, who giggled just as much every time she told the story—well girls, you really can't begin to guess. . . . He turned me over like a pancake on his bed, so flustered and hurried that he sort of mixed everything up, he thought the back was the front and as he got up he said: You see, you little pretender, you weren't a virgin, but all the same a person couldn't fit Apollinaire's hundred-thousand virgins in there—Jesus, I was eternally grateful to Apollinaire, for eight whole days I couldn't sit down, and the real kicker was that I was still a virgin and that I was going to find myself burdened with the grim task of giving this little present to one of my darling fiancés in the high rises. I got my bikers' shoes, plus three or four other pairs, Chantelle stockings and a whole supply of socks that Vlad brought every time by the dozen in his little suitcase, with diamonds, with squares, in shetland wool, in cashmere.... After which, leaving the Home Sweet Home after my first go-round, I felt the bills rustling in my bag, stirred by the light breeze of the thoughts racing through my mind, I was a little wobbly on my feet because of the whiskey and Seti the First, and my ass was hurting but I felt higher than the Himalayas and all the kites in China.

*

Abel had, like Hughette, the courage of his passions—that is, writing and pederasty, vices to which he dedicated his life in equal measures. After having given philosophy classes in Pollès, the diploma mill for daddies' girls, he renounced once and for all any contact with society, which didn't stop him from now and then looking for a small job, scribbling out bills in an insurance company, getting laid off and signing up for unemployment to receive the eight-hundred franc monthly allotment which meant that he did not have to be completely supported by Hughette.

—I hope he didn't bring his cute young thing back like last time, Hughette said, emptying her purse on the landing to look for her key. Or his buddy Marco, a Buster Keaton type in Snow White drag. Last Saturday I had gone to get my grandmother at the Gare de Lyon, and seeing how she was supposed to spend a few days in Paris I had no choice but to let her stay here, so I had made tea, stashed away everything that looked weird, scratched suspicious stains off the bed— and I get here and find the door double-locked. Surprised,

I knock, no answer, I take out my key which by some miracle I hadn't forgotten, I open the door a crack and what do I see: Abel stark naked in bed with a little lovebird. Red lights, smell of hash, curtains drawn at four in the afternoon; you can imagine my grandmother's expression, in her grocery store in Marseilles you don't see something like that every day. So, real cool I throw open the curtains, the window, I empty the ashtrays, I boil some water, asking Granny whether she wants Chinese or Ceylonese. The lovebird slipped out through the service entrance, duds in hand probably. For a whole week I pretended Abel wasn't there. He was unhappy, poor guy, he couldn't sleep, he told me it was a real pain in the ass to take Dulcinea to a hotel; in short, he softened my heart. But then, the final blow was that Abel noticed that the darling boy had gone through his pockets, plus made off with his pullovers. The woes of love. Serves you right, I told him, only you got to keep your grubby paws out of where . . . well, in the place I keep my savings. All you got to do is ask. Everybody gets had sooner or later, right?

*

With Abel I madly drifted through the fourth dimension of an unknown cosmos, inhabited by onyx-eyed unicorns, poet pederasts, whores with python-like bodies, phalluses made of barley sugar, and philanthropic cops. Abel wrote apocalyptic poems that he went off to bellow at midnight on the rue Saint-Benoît to collect loose change in his feathered felt hat, but unfortunately hearing that the end of the world was galloping ever closer howled out in alexandrines ended up by grating on the nerves of Christians who bombarded the police station with telephone calls until the order was passed on to the owner of the Malene bistro to send Abel to the clink where nobody would ever have gone through the trouble to get him, except for Hughette, who brought him back by the scruff of his neck, hollering—everybody knows the world's done for, that's no reason to keep people from sleeping, and what's more all I'm good for is to go retrieve the genius when checkmate time rolls round.

But I really adored Abel. At last an adult who talked our language. Once we started him going on childhood, it was impossible to shut him up.

The days there were shakedowns at home; we got to Hughette's with our tails between our legs, we threw our attaché cases into a corner and we turned the TV on without saying a word. That's when Abel sensed the drama, the thunder started to roll, and we were ecstatic; we let Abel baby talk us while we whined that our papers had been rummaged through, everything thrown topsy-turvy to find what, for Christ's sake? The Great Secret. The elixir of eternal life. In fact our mothers really didn't know what they were looking for, but their police dog instincts put them on a trail scented with hashish, freedom, sunlight, provocative odors that had to be neutralized with a few sprays of Air-Wick and insecticide.

Obviously, Abel roared, they'd open up your stomachs just like that to auscultate your livers like Roman augurs, they'd shoot you up with truth serum in your asses, they'd put you into a drugged stupor and then lock you away in the bughouse. They're all the same, those walking ovaries. What gives them the right, tell me, all because they kept a seed warm for nine months. I'll tell you: every right. There they go as powerful as Rhea the Earth herself, no sooner they've popped out their string bean, the gumdrop they're going to knead for fifteen years until it takes the shape they like—more often than not they knead while looking at themselves in the mirror. Hey, he's got my hair and my eyes, grandmother's nose, just a smidge of the ears and ass of his daddy, and the navel that's me again, that navel is in my spitting image—and Mommy has ecstatic orgasms squeezing the little princess in her arms, it's even more sickening if it's Sonny Boy. Come here, tell Mommy you love her snookums, come tell me in Aztec, in Chinese, in Kirghiz, come in between the sheets, it's so warm, and blow your nose down there where nothing can ever hurt you anymore because I'm here, my womb, that fortress of silence still remembering the echoes of its glory when your pretty little toesies drummed inside so hard I thought they were going to break the viscous barrier protecting you, my love, as my arms do now. That's one side of the coin. Different side, different tone.

The little darling has got to stick to the image they have of him or her. A superimposed life. And look how the kid's shadow is getting bigger, longer, is becoming enormous—how mommy's is shrinking away. This can't be. Enraged, stamping with their heels on the edges of the shadow, tortured like an oyster by a squirt of lemon juice, shrinking back with a moan to the required dimensions. Go take a nap, I'm sleepy, put on a vest, I'm cold. And mommy galloping after her pride and joy in full flight, to catch him squirming all around and force him into the woolen cardigan that she knitted herself, reeking of suint and patience.

Second story: In my parents' garden, in Moret-sur-Loing, a cherry tree had been planted that belonged all to me. People said: Abel's cherry tree. Unfortunately, it stayed scraggly; at every frost it almost died the terrible death of trees, and had NEVER borne a single cherry, a sure symbol

of the life awaiting me; in short, damn it, all that I wanted
was to stuff my face with my cherries from my cherry tree.
So my parents put on a little act more for their amusement
than mine, in which the maid Ginette came in with her
hands empty at dessert time and feebly said: Oh, I'm so sorry
for you, Monsieur, there's no fruit at all in the garden . . . the
sparrows ate them all, or the little hoodlums next door
filched them this morning. But surely you've forgotten
Abel's cherry tree, my father said, indeed you know the one,
the small tree at the back of the garden, last row. Of course!
Ginette exclaimed. I dash out to see if there are any. The
outcome of the quest was awaited with a religious silence,
my father twisting his mustache, my mother casting a
pitying look upon me until Ginette enters triumphantly
bearing a plate of cherries bought that very morning at the
market. You see what superb bigaroons there are on Abel's
cherry tree, my father said. And at the age of five, I learned to
lie in order not to disappoint them and to conform to their
implacable conception of childhood dopiness. What's
more, if that shitty excuse for a tree had borne something, it
most certainly would not have been bigaroons but tiny,
acidy balls that would have made a barely edible compote—
but it had as much chance to bear cherries as a plane tree or
a silver birch.

  — That's funny, Hughette said, I never had the impression
I was being lied to. But we don't come from the same world.
I lived in a Marseilles high rise with my three sisters and my
two brothers, I was the oldest, and every time my mother
decided to have an abortion I was the one who helped her;
Friday nights the doc came around with his probe, the
uterus had time to go into convulsions during the weekends
and Sunday it evacuated all on its own, and I took it off to the
trashcan wrapped in a newspaper. On Monday mornings
she opened the grocery store at eight sharp. So as far as truth

goes, I got it smack in my face every single day, gothic novels, soap operas, the dad who comes home loaded and starts beating, kids huddled in their corners listening to the floor squeak when he got in at night. So you can all cry all you want about having a cushy life when you were kids.

You want to talk about the ratafia of childhood memories, so let's talk. Mornings back home in Marseilles, my father would come to give my little brother Angelo a shove; he threw him out of bed hollering, Shine my shoes, you little shitass, slob, good for nothing, bum, bastard, jailbird, snoring away the day like that you'll sure as hell never be able to earn one penny, it's in the cards you'll end up in prison, when I think how I slaved away so you could get your diploma, look at my reward—a diploma, sure, Angelo had his electrician's certificate. But you've been through the Coué method. Thanks to hearing the old man repeat the same bullshit, he did end up as people predicted—right at this very moment he's got room and board in a Baumettes jail cell. Before sentencing, I was scared they would lock him up in a nuthouse. My brother's a wacko. When he had his fits, I often thought he was going to choke the old man to death. One day he got fed up taking all those kicks in the ass; he split from home just about the same time as I did, and life really began. There was this whole gang he was leader of. A really well-organized thing, a genuine association with headquarters in a bar on rue Lodi and a warehouse in a garage near the Canebière. When they got nabbed, in the trunk of their car the cops found a Mauser, duplicate keys, chloroform, a billy club, a ski mask, a jimmy, a screwdriver and a stencil for repainting license plates. I got to say Angelo is real crazy about the movies. He learned everything from American flicks. Nothing scared him, he produced some real-life screenplays, he had his personal team in hand, he aimed for the major department stores, hotels, villas, nothing but the best. He wouldn't have started the ball rolling for a measly two francs fifty like his brother Raymond—I'd rather not talk about that guy. If he hadn't been really paranoid, Angelo might have put enough dough on the side to take it easy until he retired. Well, that was all a dream, because he blew everything any way he could. At any rate, the night they had decided to break into a lawyer's place, some villa in a suburb of Marseilles, I smelled something dangerous in the air. You're on the rag, you're on edge, that's what he told me. Then they were off. The job looked like a cinch, nobody living close by and just a garage door to force open. Rich people give the impression they want to get burglarized, like they feel guilty about having too much money. Well, I don't know what got into Angelo's buddies that night, but they really screwed up. It was just too easy until then. Their last job, breaking into the Prisunic in Bandol, made the papers. Fame and Glory. The third Thursday in Lent a gang of criminal youths gained entry to the Prisunic and swiped fifty big ones from the register—but what those reporters didn't know was that the night watchman didn't lift a finger to stop them; he even yelled, Take everything, that will leave less for the fascists to put into their own pockets! So they politely offered him a beer that they pinched from the food section before, tying him to a chair so he wouldn't get into any trouble with his boss—they said he absolutely wanted to follow them, he cried into his bottle of Tuborg. You'll never guess what they made off with, beside the contents of the register: six-hundred pairs of extra-sheer nylon stockings, a hundred and twenty nightshirts and two-hundred slips— all for their sisters—plus a stack of Elvis Presley records.

—What about the lawyer?

—Right, the lawyer. They smashed up everything in the study. Lawyers turned their stomachs; they stunk of hearses and tombs. Every time Angelo thought about lawyers, he thought about inheritances, family trees. Rummaging through the files left out on the lawyer's desk, he runs right into a will which he starts to read out loud to his pals, just for laughs, then reaching the codicil he goes totally white. Without that damned codicil, three lines at the end of the page, he would have finished a lot sooner. Disinheriting your kids, he howled, isn't that a disgrace, pigs, degenerates, bastards—the others tried to shut him up, but it was hopeless, he kept ranting and raving, sons of bitches every last one of them, roaches, they can just wait and see how it'll all go up in flames this pile of slop, and striking a match and setting the papers on fire, the curtains catch, alarms, firemen, cops, they were barely able to save them.

You see, that will belonged to a father who wasn't leaving his son a dime. And that father might well have been his if he had had any dough. So Angelo's whole childhood rises to his throat, he's choked with anger, he has a fit, a kind of epilepsy, but that doesn't stop him from getting slapped with two years minimum. I'm afraid he won't make it through to the end. Last month he swallowed a whole pack of pins to get it all over with; all he managed to do was give his tummy a tickle. I even screw up my own suicide, is what he told me after.

Poor guy, Abel said. That makes the third time Hughette has told me the story of her brother and it gets to me every time. I weep like an old crocodile, I feel like my mother is reading *Les Misérables* to me. Well, anyway, if everything works out, when would your public enemy get out of prison?

—In July, Hughette said. What a day of celebration. But I hope he can keep going until then. I'm going to see he really lives it up on the Riviera, that'll get him back on his feet, wait and see . . .

At that point Hughette's eyes lit up in a way that made you

feel good all over. Living it up with Angelo. . . . So easy to imagine. Springtime, freedom, going down south by car, pockets crammed with money, enough to pay for a suite at the Majestic in Cannes, at the Negresco in Nice or at the Hôtel de Paris in Monte Carlo. . . .

The coolest thing about the palaces, Hughette said, was breakfast. I had my first luxury breakfast at the Georges V, after a backbreaking night with an Arabian sheik. I really deserved my croissants. When I'm in the money, every morning will be like that: my governess will come put the tray on the bed for me—a big silver tray, with such a heap of pots and pitchers on top you haven't the slightest inkling what they're for, teapots with elaborate spouts and handles, all of it polished to death so that it sparkles and shines; here, look, I collect these, little milk pitchers, every chance I steal one, this is a masterpiece, look at that one, the perfectly smooth and shapely edge—okay, so it's not practical, you never manage to finish the milk, there's always some going bad at the bottom, but still, a pitcher like that makes you feel good—take Hollywood swimming pools, now I don't want a damn thing to do with them; for me the good life means little trifles like this, a breakfast tray, coffee drunk from porcelain cups so fine you see the daylight through them, it tastes different, it's even stronger and blacker—and little spoons, I got a pile of them, they're easy to snitch, but if it wasn't so awkward to carry I'd be off with the whole service every chance I'd get.

And Hughette, very proud, took out from her dresser drawers her complete collection of spoons and milk pitchers, arranged with the obsessive devotion of butterfly collectors or fetishists who hide socks in their closets that they masturbate with, because this disparate silverware represented, in her mind, the future she was hoping for, made up of late mornings spent in bed in a satin nightgown, embroidered mule slippers on her feet, smoking Bensons, the cigarettes wrapped in gold, while she took little sips of her slowly drip-brewed coffee, alternately reading *The Marchioness of the Angels* and *The Psychopathology of the Rat* in three volumes—things that didn't have the slightest appeal for me whatsoever, and I treated her like a repressed middle-class matron, but it's true that I had always slept, until then, on feather pillows, and as far as the cushy life went, I really had nothing, and I mean nothing, to do with it anymore.

ONDINE: I must say, I am so very happy to discover that men are so beautiful. . . . My heart has almost stopped beating! . . .
AUGUSTE: Be quiet!
ONDINE: I'm shivering all over!
AUGUSTE: She's fifteen, dear knight. Excuse her . . .

Jean Giraudoux, *Ondine*

Thanks to hearing Hughette talk to me about her brother Angelo, little by little my passion crystallized for the will-burning hero, the great pin swallower—you only fall in love with myths, and Angelo represented nothing less than those of Arsène Lupin, Stavisky and Cartouche all wrapped up in one. At night, in my dreams, I galloped upon a small Arabian horse across the great *kavirs* of Iran, scattered here and there with the skulls and shins of buffalo perfectly polished by the blowing sand, I dashed through tragic deserts where only the lamentation of parents and distraught ancestors came to disturb the silence, a dying complaint issuing from the faraway, intermediary kingdom of Khorva where man is dead or as yet unborn, a song of uncertainty rising from a labyrinth of boredom where an exhausted Ariadne did not even unravel her ball of thread anymore to help poor humans make their way out of the place, a curved hyperbolic melody, an abstract warbling like the muezzin's at noon, a music of despair with no beginning or end, like the vine branches of jade and the azure foliage encircling the cupolas of mosques.

Getting off my nag, I walked toward the tinkling grove of an oasis where Angelo was waiting to kiss me with the mad violence of Rudolph Valentino in *The Son of the Sheik.*

*

A kiss: I couldn't get my mind off of it. I fed on immaterial kisses the whole blessed day long. A real obsession. That first kiss was something that could only be exchanged in exceptional surroundings like the Place des Fêtes on a foggy day, or the hall of a train station, preferably the Gare du Nord's—what could be more like an aphrodisiac than a train station, people only passing through, a place of gray light, soot, tears, smoke and muck where the poisonous particles of cooled ash get into your nostrils and leave an iron taste on your lips, cathedrals of rust and coal where the echoes of an international pidgin resonate—Schlafwagen Speisesaal diningroum e pericoloso sporghesi—and where the Orient-Trans-Europ-Express, the Trains Bleus and the Harmonika Zug sleep in the cold light of the leaded windows; we would sneak into a compartment, throw one of those scratchy French railroad blankets over our heads, we wouldn't take a breath until the whistle blew and wheels began to turn, and the knowing train would charge into the tunnel of initiation that swallows children and sucks them into its black cacophony of screeching spirits only to spit them out again into the daylight, adults at last, free to toss

their kiddy rags out of the window and to dance stark naked
in the corridor where bars of sunlight tremble, ingots of
sunshine, the chalky sun of the morning of the last metamorphoses.

Or else—to get back to the first kiss—it would happen
right after sticking up a Prisunic, like in Bandol. A super-
Prisunic. Let's say a shopping mall. Hands up and nobody
move—certainly not, the night watchman says, get going,
hurry, don't forget the caviar and the watches—after a lightning raid we jump into the cars and there Angelo, raising his
carnival mask, kisses me and lifts my schoolgirl's skirt, oh
come on, no point in dawdling, a fourteen-year-old Romeo
that's Juliet's age, let him plow into me up to my liver like a
Malayan kris, let me bleed, so much the better if it runs as
hot as only my mother's tears could, and the gold chain
snapped between Salammbô's ankles when Matho spread
her thighs, and I under the folds of starry zaïmph on the
backseat of the Aronde I pay for my liberty with a good pint
of blood—Australian aborigines impale girls to divirginate
them, to remove this humiliating and pathetic bolt, because
those savages still know that blood speaks of a cruel shattering existence in which men live the instinctive life of
animals undergoing metamorphoses—I also know, splattered with immortality, changed into a dakînî, forehead
struck with the third eye, a vampire with wings of
membranous felt, I who am in the process of crossing
through the third rite of passage, still remembering the first
—one day I was thrust out of a slit spreading slowly like a
theater curtain, I see men in white who look like they're
expecting me, I suddenly got very cold with the impression
of being ejected like slag from a volcanic crater—then
blood stained my sheets and I became a cavern, a cave and
depth—today from the laceration of the night ran a red pain
spotting the cushions of the Aronde and dripping onto the

world, Angelo dared not move anymore for fear of aggra-
vating the disaster that was really raining down, a little
puddle was forming on the ground, it's going to show
through the plaid, I said faintly, try to find a hankie to use as a
tampon, I'd sure like to, Angelo says, but if I budge it'll hurt
you, uhh, I say, I don't have the impression it could get any
worse, this vagina problem must have been something completely unexpected, just my own little anomaly. Relax,
Angelo says. I'm trying, I say. We've got to manage, can't put
it off till tomorrow and anyway, Angelo, I love the soft lock
of your bangs so much, like a bird-of-paradise feather hiding
your eyes when you exert yourself, like when you're playing
pinball; the morning alarm, here I am blasted back into false
reality, the mirrors have turned about abruptly like the
turnstile of the Café de la Paix and nobody has come to snap
the chain.

*

While waiting, I was still dealing with the kiss, the first stage
of discovery, a complicated slobbery thing whose user's
manual is nowhere to be found. In movies they say people
just pretend. According to Polline, that pathological liar
who had a good lead over me because of the forbidden
games she gave herself over to in her cellar and the fact she
read *The 120 Days of Sodom,* it was all a matter of opening
your mouth like a carp, inserting your tongue into your
partner's mouth, twisting it like a screw, after which, big
mystery! If Angelo ever tried, I was going to come off like a
royal ass. So I started to look under the nose of every male
specimen that came into view, the concierge's son, the ap-
prentice butcher and Schmauz's brother; if I had the guts I

would have pushed back their upper lips the way you do
with stallions, but shy creature that I was, I made do with
comparing the firmness of the mucus membrane, the coloring of the tooth enamel, and gums.

In retrospect, kissing is still the thing I believe is most
essential. The real act of love. You can fuck a whore, but you
don't kiss one on the mouth. Tristan and Isolde, Romeo and
Juliet, Héloïse and Abélard, Vivien Leigh and Clark Gable in
Gone with the Wind, spent all their time kissing on the lips
until they practically suffocated. They hardly survived in-
between time. You've got to learn to discriminate between
kisses, do a lot of experimenting, and it's like caviar or
Bordeaux—in the beginning you don't have any apprecia-
tion since your taste buds aren't developed. At that time I
didn't know there was such a tremendous variety—well-
behaved kisses, kisses rough to the touch, round-edged
kisses, dry and pointy kisses, wet kisses, loose-lipped kisses,
toothy kisses and tonguey kisses, mucous kisses and ivory
kisses, open and closed kisses, exploratory kisses that poke
around all the way behind the barrier of the incisors and
insinuate themselves in the silky grotto of the palate,
tongue-scraping kisses, face-washing kisses, reactionary and
revolutionary kisses, titillating kisses, spidery kisses, polite
kisses, honey cough-drop kisses, Cartesian kisses, knowing
kisses, innovative kisses, avant-garde kisses—and the
elementary kiss, the fatal kiss, the kind that isolates you all at
once in the middle of a magnetic field flushed with astral
light, the essential organic kiss wherein the saliva secretes a
fateful fluid, the dope of cruelty in your veins, the discharge
of the absolute in your blood, the catalyst of flowing liquids,
the kiss charged with the black power ruling the nuptial
migrations of birds, the host kiss abolishing time, the kiss
sealed within a distressing quest for the unformed, the
bardo of time, the sacred bite, the pact between blood and

deep waters—for a kiss like that, just one, I'd trade in, along with all the other kisses, every single erotic refinement of the Ananga Ranga and even the mercurial tumble of pleasure at the bottom of your belly.

*

One day the doctor's probe missed its ovule and Raymond began to prosper in Hughette's mom's belly, a fetus predestined for flops, reckless skids, and general catastrophe. That's what Raymond was, an accident. Even as a baby, he caught on to this right off, and started out by refusing to cry like other infants. The result was that he was pumped with oxygen like a tire and stuck into an incubator which he came out of convinced that, since he was in surplus, all he had to do was make himself as small as possible so as not to be too much of a bother. At age seventeen he was only four-foot-eleven, including his boot heels, which he got custom-made at Lobb's, costing him an arm and a leg.

—Raymond's a real washout, Hughette said. He wasn't in Paris two weeks before he got himself hauled off to jail for ripping off two packages of noodles. A disaster of a hoodlum, I'm telling you. When he finds an old lady to keep him, he winds up reimbursing her for the money she slipped him. His hobby is antiques. Like he's got a castle to deck out in Louis Treize.

Polline, sensitive soul, was already harboring feelings of tender protectiveness for Raymond when one fine day he showed up in the flesh, striding into the midst of the heavenly choirs, a halo in the shape of a little gold crepe floating above his head that is not all that high in relation to the floor, and the very instant he walked into the room I discerned a muttering inside Polline's head in which the names of Napoleon and others of history's Lilliputian geniuses kept turning up, which forced me to choke off the "still-and-all a real hedgehopper" itching right on the tip of my tongue, and to flash the midget a smile riddled with dimples and polished with a pearly gloss which hurt my cheeks, thanks to my perfecting it.

Raymond was carrying a rectangular package that he started to unwrap in front of us. Get a look at this thing, he said. An eighteenth-century fireplace screen. When you think how people just chuck them out. Sixteenth-century cellars are packed with these splendors. Those degenerates buy Knoll and toss all the old furniture on the scrap heap. The next time I make the rounds, I'm bringing along Abel, who knows what's what. Oh, you know, Abel said, I'd be scared of getting sick in your catacombs. Then Polline, who had been squirming in her seat the whole while trying to attract attention, gets up and shouts: What about me, ever think of taking me, just for once? a question which set into motion the Dark Forces of Western Passion, caused a multi-star pileup and a spectacular snap-to of Raymond's spine, and he abruptly started to grow a few inches.

— Here, he said to Polline, take the screen, it's for you. I'll get some andirons to go with.

I could already see our parents' expressions before a pair of rocaille shepherdesses, wall lamps and other trinkets stored away by chance in our bedrooms, but Polline, who had only one place to stick the andirons, that fireplace in Bailleul where there wasn't much to be protected from in the way of fire, without the slightest protest would have let the guy palm off on her a church pulpit or even a writing desk, provided it made Raymond happy who, his neurons short-circuited, was teetering on the wispy bases of his Lobb heels.

*

From the moment he met Polline, Raymond went on a genuine kleptomaniacal spree: Dupont lighters, Hermès scarves, cans of caviar and other trifles; price was no object when it came to making his honey happy. And plus, she whispered blissfully, he wanted to take her to America, the States—Land of Milk and Honey, a miraculous land loaded with dough and hamburgers, watered with rivers of ketchup, bristling with cacti on which lynxes grew as in the Living Desert, Disney-wonderland where geysers of oil shot up, squirts of which trickled back on Scarlett O'Hara's dress, and where cops patted you on the fanny while taking drags on their joints, a land without rules, beside the Constitution's, which was nobody's concern but the President's.

One Thursday, Raymond took us to the Drugstore, a fully realized world at last, a coded universe off-limits to adults, and decipherable by using words, for starters, like *rock, banana split, extra, shetland, boots,* and *parties,* inhabited by a new race of mutants whose comings and goings we gawked at with our eyes as wide open as the teacups of Andersen's dog: cute guys in their Renoma uniforms. The girls especially fascinated me, so artificial that I felt like crumpling them in my fingers like crepe paper camellias or felt butterflies, and I felt like spreading apart the stiff, opaque bangs brushing against the edges of their false mink eyelashes, just to see if a forehead was hiding under that fringe, and I felt like baring their mouths, indiscernible through a layer of beige lip gloss, and I felt like scraping off those gobs of plaster that made their faces look like Noh theater masks or porcelain coated with a thick glaze; I ate myself up with desire before their outfits, making myself a promise that one day I too would have a Scottish kilt with a huge safety pin whose delicate pleats would flutter around my knees, white lace stockings with little flowers and moccasins with tassels. Lucien de Rubempré strolling in the Tuileries did not feel crummier upon seeing Rastignac pass by than I did in my little curly lamb's-wool coat faced with these afficionados of perfection. Perhaps I was going to get a glimpse of Fisher or Papazian, those pillars of the Drugstore, metamorphosed after passing through the doors of the Monaco, the café at the Chateaudun intersection, from which they emerged pollinated all over with Caron powder on their way up to the Drugstore, only to repeat the procedure in the reverse face-scrubbing sense before they set foot back in their parents' homes.

*

We lost no time getting into the habit of going to the Drugstore with Raymond on Thursdays, Saturdays, and Sunday afternoons. Our visits were scheduled for around three o'clock, after at great length bringing together all the members of the gang who then decided either to crash a party in the sixteenth arrondissement or to set up camp in one of the nightclubs in the area, Whiskey Sour, Pappy Club, Berlingot and especially the Relais de Chaillot, smoky reddish chthonian places where at the door we left work, school, squares, truths rinsed in Omo and the whole litany of Don'ts, to get one over on the Filthy Mess of the day and discover in the make-believe night the fabulous flirting game, the interplay of shadows, of lies, the game of luck, of competition, the only one whose rules we knew by instinct.

Thursday night, eight o'clock. Well, is Robert Hirsch good
in *Les Fourberies de Scapin?* Mom asks naively, setting the
plate of veal marengo on the table. Schemes, let's talk about
them. Was she laying a trap for me? Maybe the Comédie-
Française burned down, or Hirsch broke a leg on the stairway and he was rushed to the hospital, with big headlines in
Le Figaro. I pick off a tiny bit of veal, cursed animal, and
grumble an indistinct answer, something stupid and
unintelligible, a marengo answer. That's nice, Mom says—
then turning to my father: Listen, Antoine, about the pay . . .
Fine, it's all right, the rockets have stopped whistling in my
ears, I can swiftly telescope myself down inside and go back
to the Pierre Charron. I will never forget going into the
Pierre Charron, lit by a red lamp, the color of danger and
whorehouses, and the steep stairway—below, paradise
flipped direction, made an abrupt about-face and sent hell
flying into the upper regions. The angel Gabriel sells tickets
for ten francs apiece at the top of the stairs, and the Garden
of Eden is off-limits to children under eighteen, it's written
above the door that you need a card to get past, but with
Raymond we make it past the danger without any problem.
We'll get our school IDs faked, Polline whispers to me,
because with these raids you never know.

Below, in the darkness, a swarm of extras mills about, all
done up glossy, pretty, satiny with long clean hair that only
half hid their cruising glances. Not a single seat. Kids
ranging from fourteen to twenty, all over the place,
standing, on the floor, on the stairs, on the arms of chairs, in
the black corners—no way to get a toe in edgewise over
there. In the middle, on a floor lit by a real movie projector, a
slew of dudes is doing the "letkiss" holding each other's
arms, heel to toe, and we clap our hands. Adventure music,

the "big game," broken rules, this is where it is all happening. Only Angelo is missing; if he were holding my hand to plow us through the crowd I would feel like I was trotting along behind Caesar's or Alexander's chariot, and I would find him even more handsome in other people's eyes. The string of slow dances starts, the spotlights go out, here and there groups come together, then apart, those dudes must be hemeralopic to ferret out the girl they like in the total darkness; here and there lighters flick on and their slender flames light a three-quarters profile powdered dull white. Jesus, Papazian. The slut's unrecognizable in that red lipstick whose sheen is like a heavenly snail's slime or the inside of an oyster shell still polished by ocean water, her eyes darkened with kohl, as brilliant as two mica-rich lakes stagnating in the heart of a primeval carboniferous forest, and that tight lamé pullover, its gold and silver blossoms molding her small braless breasts—Winston smoke exhaled from her porcelain nostrils twists in baleful rings like sulfur burned at the feet of Black Kali; no kidding, if I was a guy I'd have gone off my rocker for Papazian, queen of the heavy breathers, who claims sixty flings to her credit just for 1964, maybe she's getting a little carried away, but still. No sooner she spots me with Raymond and Polline than she makes a beeline toward me and pulls me into a corner. Well, well, she says. Little Lydie. How about this, you're emancipating yourself. Just a guy from the Drugstore, no big deal. He's not mine, I say, he's Pauline's. What luck, Papazian says. Take me, I met up with still another zero, get a look at this telephone number, AVI something or other, AVI ary AVI, it must be another of those suburban dumps—you'd need radar to detect a PASSY right off in this darkness. My problem is that I always meet up with prizes from the Championnet-Goutte d'or gang. Never fails, either that or else straight-out hicks from the high rises, Asnieres and that whole crowd. Well then, she adds humbly, which made me blush with pride, don't forget who your girlfriends are, I'm counting on you to introduce me around.

Living Dangerously

"Live dangerously and hit the road."
—André Breton

The Drugstorian spring frittered away between the Etoile, the Scossa, the Pierre Charron and the Relais de Chaillot from three to six, Thursdays, Saturdays and Sundays. This time it was really worth the trouble to slave over our alibis. The Comédie-Française, the Planetarium, and the Musée de l'Homme were no longer enough to set our parents at ease who, through a sort of sixth sense, even though we were always careful to scour ourselves thoroughly in the toilets of the Monaco before going back home with Fisher and Papazian, sniffed suspicious whiffs of tobacco and Molinard perfume around us. So we progressed to visits to the catacombs, the sewers, the National Archives, Musée de l'Armée, the Carnavalet, the Conciergerie and even, driven by a sudden love for stamp collecting, the Post Office Museum.

Leaving home like that was okay, just showoff, but when it came to running away, the idea never crossed our minds. Nothing's more exhausting than running away, the very idea of which made us feel like hitting the sack and sometimes brought on nasty consequences like a short stay in Savignysur-Orge, a special brand of Youth Activity Center where, to hear people tell it, the mental scoliosis afflicting our generation was set right. Run the risk of seeing yourself locked away just for acting up a little, what would ever possess you? On the other hand, we couldn't give a damn about the ideological struggle, which got us labeled as the middle class in the eyes of Cloclo and her crowd, while at the same time we were coming across like depraved anarchists to the straight chicks in school. In short, we didn't have enough motivation to run away, no more three afternoons of delights each week—I would have agreed to work like a dog and not see sunlight six days out of seven, provided that I reexperience the smell of Sundays at Polline's, the smell of polish, of hair scorched by her grandmother's curling iron that we used—for the opposite effect, to stiffen it until it formed a small, snug-fitting helmet over our heads—the smell of Bourdaloue quiches being reheated in the oven, mingling with stubborn traces of Fawn's Kiss perfume with which we methodically rubbed our seven orifices following Tseu-hi's beauty tips, the last empress of China, one fabulous lady whose spells were brought to us by Pearl Buck, who had fully tried and tested them.

It took an incredibly earthshaking conjunction of events to disturb our exquisite undercover existence. Let me give the details. At the top was the Champs-Elysées, the Drugstore. At the bottom, the Pub Renault. Between the two, the vast plain where battles were mercilessly waged, an epic backdrop against which love stories modeled after Shakespeare came to a climax, usually settled by monumental rumbles, just as political questions concerning territorial defense were elsewhere.

Well, one Thursday, I refused to go along with Raymond and Polline to a party on Avenue de Friedland. Major event. You're dropping me, says Polline, dismayed. Well, kid, look, if it's just to hold a candle, I reply, that doesn't do a thing for me. I've got other ambitions than stuffing my face with petits fours while you feel each other up way down in some deep sofa. I'm going off to Avenue Marceau with a guy from the Pub—do unto others as you would others do unto you, the grass is always greener, evil be to her who evil thinks—bye-bye.

If I hadn't knocked down several goblets of champagne and flirted with three guys in a row, if the first of the three hadn't been jealous and above all smashed, my initiative probably wouldn't have spilled over onto the future course of events; the only thing was, dude number one, miffed in his rotten phallocratic pride, stuck me into a storage room with four of his buddies who would have screwed me pronto if Raymond hadn't arrived along with some tough numbers from the Drugstore who really gave them the once-over before yanking me out of there by the scruff of my neck—that'll teach you to hang around with cruds, Raymond concluded, tossing me like a package into a taxi next to Polline, looking real sorry and sympathetic.

After all this commotion it was eight o'clock when I rang at my door, blackout time, and I barely had a second to work out all the details of a vague song-and-dance: tea at the Grande Cascade with Papazian, evening coming on, guys in black leather who jumped us, nobody in sight, fight, running like mad, finding a taxi by some miracle—Heurtebise himself at the wheel arriving to rescue the lost immortals. Yeah. When I walked into the dining room, the broth was already cooling in the plates, and in its eyes, the broth's, I saw the future glinting the color of murky dishwater. I started to come out with my little tale, and the broth's eyes wrinkled in merriment, but not my mother's, transformed by anger into a puffed-up cockatoo whose feathers swelled with a cataleptic fury, nor my father's, as cheerful as the

Phantom of the Opera who, without waiting for the end of my spiel, turned the radio knob and became absorbed by the news and chomped at his stew the whole time, while Geneviève Tabouis uttered her pompous predictions over the air in an ectoplasmic voice still trembling from the terrors of the year 1000. Having had it with eyeballing the broth, I concentrated (following my favorite mental yoga exercise borrowed from Zen Buddhism) on a nifty painted paper bouquet, a clump of reeds and rushes in which I sought refuge like chaste Suzanna surprised while bathing, hoping in this way to reassemble the troops of my wits dispersed in the Waterloo of my consciousness so as to avoid the definitive routing.

—Your friend Papazian has an ear infection, I don't know if you're aware, my father says, a sentence which stirs up within the softened phosphorus of my brain never-ending echoes ringing as loudly as those from a bag of marbles scattered on the floor and bouncing from the top of the stairs.

—An ear infection with parasynthetic complications, my mother adds for emphasis while passing the camembert.

With parasynthetic complications. I was a goner. I got my paw caught in the trap; the Autonomous National Bureau of the Tracks of Destiny was going to come charging over me at the speed of a locomotive; I had just fallen like an innocent flake into the woeful teeth of the great Snowplow of Order.

*

After spending a night in my dad's den, where he swore he was going to grill me until the sun came up even if it meant not getting any sleep at all, I broke down in the end and confessed that some people I didn't know took me along with them, and by pure accident I wound up at somebody's place I had never seen before where some kids roughed me up a little but nothing serious—and as for what they looked like, oh, hard to say, average height, brown hair, uhh. . . . Maybe they were wearing ski masks, my father said with a snicker. You're not going to get out of it so easy, honey, I'm going to pop over to the Larbauds' to fill them in on this latest adventure, I'd really be surprised if your dear friend Polline isn't all mixed up in this mess.

And all hell broke loose at the doctor's when, after shoving his speculum up my pussy about as delicately as if he were prying off a cap with a bottle opener, he announced that he wouldn't exactly swear on his life that I was still a virgin. This plunged the whole family into the most dire uncertainty, which I was really careful not to dispel, my lips sealed shut and snickering deep down inside over this catastrophe just so I wouldn't break down in tears.

I quickly gathered that the major issue that preoccupied my parents wasn't so much the loss of my precious virginity, because in an emergency you can always get yourself another, but rather its inevitable consequence: pregnancy, a process whose results, to hear adults talk, seemed as inescapable as the punishment for selling your brother for a plate of lentils. A genuine time bomb. According to my mother's theories, a nice young lady from a proper family was sure to get knocked up no sooner than a male pecker brushed the top of her thigh and even if she kept her virginity, she might still get nabbed, like a crook, by some roving sperm cell, a real trooper that one, with a head for trouble and whose way through the triple obstacles of dress and panties with slip in-between I couldn't begin to imagine. But that was only the beginning of the fun and games; although nobody even mentioned sex to me before, all of a sudden they started stuffing me full of all this talk, both vague and precise, making precise what should be left vague and vice versa, small masterpieces of turdified obscenity that would have made me frigid for the rest of my life if I hadn't let it go in one ear and out the other, wondering what the hell all this nonsense about pools of blood and membranes and ovule had to do with our absolutely crazy cruising and our games full of hugging and violence and darkness in the shimmering shadows of the Pierre Charron movie theater. For these adult types, sex was more or less a problem of drops of sperm, testicles, the prostate gland, diaphrams, bidets and spermacide, very filthy, very complicated stuff that would put you to sleep, and had nothing in the world to do with pleasure that spread as slow and steady as a fireworks' falling sparks, blossoming under an eighteen-year-old kid's lips one bright Sunday afternoon in an apartment in Neuilly where nobody was around to be a pain in the ass, not even the maid who was watching TV, nothing in the world to do with how soft Christian's hair felt or Olivier's knowing fingers, a real master at putting on the make, nothing with the total happiness of being asked to dance by that real tall, real blonde guy that you spotted at the back of the room at the lycée Henri IV dance, nothing with our budding knowledge of telling apart all these new smells that surrounded you or assaulted you when you slow dance real tight with some strange guy you want to feel up, to breathe in, to nibble because his eyes remember what innocence is, and you feel yourself delicately ensnared in the net of the million-and-one things the stranger's touch tells you, this alien who has approached your planet and whose aura mingles with yours as slowly as a cloud drifting in front of the moon, until the moment you get that electric shock that depends on blood type, astrological sign, the quality of your complexion and pure chance, such a thrilling

blast that I wondered why people miss so many oppor-
tunities to experience it, because that's what life should be
all about, a series of skin-to-skin contacts, sensual, and
apsychological, as soon as somebody catches your eye in the
street, you should rush over to him and throw yourself in his
arms, after all, who knows, it might be a father or a fiancé
you knew and loved in some former life, and if that has
nothing whatsoever to do with what's going on at least you
have the benefit of the doubt—those eyes, they don't ring a
bell, but wait, the court in Castille, or the Montefeltre
Palace or the galleries of the Palais-Royal, that dandy
walking along using his umbrella like a knobbed cane, was
none other than the young man who crossed your path
when you were Fantasio.

In the end I really understood Hughette, who screwed
doddering old men out of simple curiosity—but me, on the
other hand, I couldn't have touched them with one finger, I
needed something smooth and brand-new for me to play
that subtle, upsetting game of Heart-scraper.

Sex, did you say? Excuse me, you're talking about the
uterus, ovaries, the penis and lubrication, don't know what
you're getting at, save those words for Molière's quacks,
they smell like church and wet-nurses' milk; why not use a
delicate or hot-and-bothered language, show us the path
True Love travels, and map out the Land of Screwing, and
Sheik Nefzaoui's scented garden, sing to us of Circe's or
Papazian's lipstick that makes you want to die for her and
compose heroic couplets on a young girl lifting her blouse
pleated like a pharaoh's kalasyris and how with a streak of
shimmering violet she speckles the hollow her thinness
carves between her breasts, sketch the fourteen-year-old
Lolita's profile, a little porcelain wall broken by the crack of
a kiss, don't obliterate the dark fragile memory of our
awkward experiences; anyway, even if you try, it'll already

be too late, nobody'll ever be able to take away that memory of the time when pop music started to make the world high, when we smoked cigarettes without inhaling just by wetting the filter in the darkness of a bowling alley on the rue de Seine, when we made phony telephone calls just so we could stay quiet at the other end of the line and catch unawares the Other's breathing, when we got smashed on pure water like those monkeys on Penang Island in Malaysia who drink themselves drunk on the water found in certain white flowers called monkey cups after snapping off the vegetal bolt that locks the calyx. Either do it that way or get right down to it. Tell us all about cunts, cocks, humping, and getting off, we'd know what you were talking about, it's hard and fast, pure, honest, clean—but as for your world where sex looks like a disease, and love's a hernia or an ulcer, your embarrassing diseases, your ladies of pleasure, your grim masturbations, the guilty pleasure of your Judeo-Christian spasms, your vulvitis, your mushy sores, your rabbit tests, you can have them, thanks, keep it all for yourself along with your dread of life, your universe of stained sheets, of guilt-ridden fags slinking along walls, of inhibited creeps, of vaginal discharges and the well-deserved pain of labor; why don't you wrap this pathetic mess up for me and throw it the hell in the Seine, and let the party start—with Angelo, of course, who I imagined standing in front of the Drugstore, let's hear some Rossini for Angelo, let me have the overture from the *Barber, La gazza ladra,* or some perverse bouncy tune like the "Musica Reservata" from the Italian sixteenth century, let the orchestra play on, lutes, horns, violas and zithers—Angelo takes a drag on his cigarette, gives it a shake and I'm the ash, in his eyes the whirl of life, behind him motorcyles roaring, under the soles of his boots a little Texas soil, under his nails a little grime and blood, in his hair a smell of pachouli and tobacco.

Right after the party incident there began a period of abstinence and reclusion that plunged us into the pit of depression. Going to see Hughette on rue Richer was now out of the question, which crushed Polline even more than me because of Raymond—she could barely get away for five minutes with the excuse of going to buy some bread and nab her guy in some back door for a quick French kiss with every move timed to the last second, after which she tore to the bakery for her bread which she bit into ferociously, a feeble outlet for her frustration.

Our mothers, who had turned into two-headed female hydras, even attempted to get around Mme. Poirier, the school principal, so that she would put us into different classes in the middle of the year, a result that was achieved in the end thanks to the vice-principal who caught Polline by surprise one day in the Saint Claude Café right in the act of tobacco-dennish inhalation with two kids from the lycée across the street and had her called into the main office from which she came out looking like Orpheus after the Bacchantes had finished with him, a black eye, a fistful of hair yanked out and a slightly loose tooth, came out and kept going because she was to be exiled immediately to the lycée La Fontaine—out in some godforsaken wilderness.

If you force the people to climb up onto barricades, you

can never be sure of getting them to come back down. This time our parents forced us to take drastic measures.

As far as their psychological motivations went, we were pretty much in the dark. We had parents with a capital *P* period—end of story. Stricken until age twelve with the astigmatism of childhood, I saw mine from too close up to make out their psychic twists and turns, whereas I could draw my late grandfather's from memory, the decorated veteran of Verdun, and my grandmother's, that archetypal woman of burden, and my spacey Aunt Ro's, all characters who were far enough removed from me so I could come up with an accurate, if not absolutely exact image, but anyway close enough to the one they liked to give of themselves. On the other hand, my mother and father were suspended in the great Void like pure astral bodies free of any failings as well as any carnal needs, their wrath was like the gods', their decisions final, their sentences never suspended, and their love, the only love that existed in a world where everything began to look like part of a plot being hatched against me.

And all of a sudden, I realized that the King and Queen of Hearts were nothing but cards, pieces of cardboard with nothing on the back, that had just been flipped around, snap, on the table, like the ones Alice picked as her judges at her trial in Wonderland before coming out with those magic demystifying words: *You're nothing but a pack of cards!*

As a matter of fact, what to our parents seemed to be some phase, a molting period, the crisis named puberty— still another poetic word—was from our point of view a static, fully realized condition, the end result of a transformation that was normal, swift and irreversible. We had grown up, we were bursting with the life we were holding in, it had been consummated; we had sliced off childhood from adolescence with our scalpel; an introverted, masochistic period was giving way to a narcissistic and rather sadistic era, and our parents could give it their best shot chasing after us with their spaying knives; we had a great head start and kept in the lead: meaning, quite a paradox. From our point of view our parents were changing. For them life wouldn't stay still; for us it was some kind of implacable monolith. We rose up against the sky as sheer and absolute as the menhirs of Karnak upon which the tempests of the ages unleashed their fury in vain.

In the meantime, their fists flew. There was nowhere to run, according to the principle that a mother must, as is right for any good enemy, be skinned alive by hand and that you could also eat her liver if you weren't afraid of getting sick.

*

So as for all that psychological squirming, guilt complex, Oedipal vipers' nests and other signs of mental decay—we didn't give a goddamn about any of it the day when, at the Tabac des Folies, we decided to go to the Riviera with Abel, Hughette and Raymond, who were going to pick up Angelo, released from prison, and then to jump onto the Orient Express, which would conduct us toward the Bosphorus— yes, but without *me,* Polline sadly says, because I haven't got a permit to leave France.

Dismay. By pure accident I was in possession of this precious scrap of paper, drawn up by my father in view of a possible stay with a German family, an eventuality which legally opened the borders of Europe for me even if the exploration of the Mainz region, rich in coal fields, did not really get my imagination's juices flowing.

After all, maybe Angelo won't really want to take you along, Polline said teasingly, while dying of jealousy. And plus you won't have a penny. Besides, he might have gotten fat and ugly; I'm sure Angelo has alveolar pyorrhea thanks to eating all that slop—I won't even mention the aerophagy because of the beans. And then walking in circles in a yard for two years, something like that must really stimulate your intellect a lot. You'll see whether your jailbird's able to speak two sentences in a row. Nothing to say? Don't give a damn about dropping me, do you? You'll just be off with your man, a wild escape, right? And me—tough out of luck.

Polline was one hell of a bore. If she was left alone for five minutes, she sulked like a dog left shut up all Sunday long in a car. Even if Angelo doesn't have any more teeth, and if gross-looking as he is he doesn't want to take me along, I'll leave all by myself, my dear pain in the ass Polline, poison mine, my hemlock root, my fly agaric, my meadow mushroom, my delicious lactescence, my phylloxera, my crumb of cheese, my harvest tick, my chrysomelid, my pieridine butterfly, my pea-weevil, my truffle for all seasons, my coca blossom—I'll hit the road because by now all I have left to me (to find out toward what sacred mountains and what seas of milk the trains, boats and planes are heading) is some thirty-thousand-and-one days.

Heavenly providence took the form of Aunt Ro, who decided in an utterly unexpected way to spend Easter vacation on the Riviera so as to keep an eye on the work being done on her house in Villefranche, leaving the camp in the hands of an agency. Considering she was somebody who could only take her sunlight in droplets upon a very green pond, and even better if it was a Seurat within a frame back in some museum, this trip down south required that she set off with a supply of deodorant, an armor of shawls, boxes of hats, and a fully panoply of Tuareg outfits destined to preserve her from the scorching heat—white especially, darling, white, above all no dark colors that hold the heat. In her medicine kit she also took some Nivaquine because of the mosquitoes crossing the Mediterranean, that insipid puddle, that bidet, on the other side of which the Land of the Darkies stretched out, named Morocco, Algeria, whatever you want, where the malaria raged that had afflicted her husband with chronic attacks during and after the war.

At the beginning of Easter week, we took the Train Bleu to go down to Villefranche, noteworthy according to the Michelin guide for the warships anchored in its port and a certain arched street dating from the High Middle Ages, under Aunt Ro's leadership, bandaged in floating scarves, her nose fitted with a blind-person's glasses and her head protected from what she called the ardors of Phoebus by a gigantic panama hat.

*

Angelo was received at the court of King Jawohl with the pomp and circumstance befitting his rank, on Easter day, and first off thought he was in the middle of some druggy high. Hardly had he stepped foot out of prison than he found himself sitting in a garden, in the midst of young girls in the first blush of youth, before a family table upon which an exquisite aunt brought the Paschal Lamb baked crusty and medium pink; there was a scent of mimosas in the air, the table wine went down real smooth and easy, good Lord it had been centuries since such a celebration had come his way, and looking at girls, isn't that a pleasure too, like food; in prison, he told Abel, you forget faces. As far as women go, all you see anymore are breasts, thighs, or backsides. But a face. Now that's something pretty. I don't believe this, you see. I'm in the middle of a dream. Plopped down in a Walt Disney movie. *Snow White* or something close. Little birds and bunnies all over the place. It can't be that this really exists. Who's the little girl at the end of the table, I didn't catch her name. Mmm? (mouthful of lamb) I'm bursting with lamb—what's that, Lydie? A girl with curls like that, a straw hat and a pink dress, I thought it was only in novels. She's real cute, she looks like a doll, I'd be afraid I'd break her, pass me the booze. And the aunt—you think I did right to kiss her hand? Really made an impression on her, huh? But what the hell are you and Hughette doing in this gingerbread house?

What I liked best about leg of lamb was the knuckle joint. But the torture you had to go through before getting your hands onto it, the plate being passed around, everybody helping themselves, grrr, the knuckle joint's still there dark golden crunchy, shit that bitch Polline's going to spot it, nope it gets away, here it is HERE IT IS all mine, what joy, I fall upon it like a bolt of lightning and one two in my plate, now things are calm, the meal can go on in peace. So nice out. Back there, Angelo, looking at me. Behind my hair, my eyelashes, my hat, I don't look like I'm looking but I am all the same. That cocksucker is some hunk. Looks a little dopey. Who wouldn't? Answers in monosyllables, sticks his nose into his lamb, or going on to Abel about who knows what, maybe about me, let's not get carried away. I should have taken the cherries off my hat, makes it look like a pie. I'm sure he hates cherries. And Aunt Ro in seventh heaven, acting real casual. Hughette, a stewardess, Abel, philosophy teacher, and the kid brother getting out of the army, she's really getting a kick out of it. A little something in Angelo's gestures totally eliminates the army hypothesis. But she pretends to believe it's true because of his hair, the way it's cut makes him look a little Gestapoish. My, my, such a scrawny mongrel, pins don't fill you out, he must have been on a hunger strike in the Baumettes. Polline ought to try pins, with vinegar, she's getting rounder now. The guy doesn't look all that crazy; just enough to be a turn-on. Those eyes. Hey, he's making a toast. To me, jeez. Chinchin, they say, I think. Or skol, that's more chic. Oh those blue South Sea eyes. A lagoon swarming with electric eels. I forget all about my knuckle joint. Provided that Ro doesn't blow it for me by saying I'm fourteen.

Our voices get louder around the table as, glass by glass, the wine goes down. Now Abel's launching into one of his grand revolutionary tirades. Whom is he talking about? Reich. Wilhelm Reich. Never heard of him.

The disappearance of social anxiety, guilt feelings and the

liquidation of the Oedipal complex, Abel says, liberates the energy linked to these fixations. So much the better. He looks like he could give a damn, Angelo does, about Wilhelm Reich. Hey, Ro approves. She's read him. She speaks. She agrees. Masturbation, Abel says. That means jerking off. They say we were all doing it from our time in the cradle. Don't remember. I really gave it a try, once, but it wore me out, you'd need a vibrator to pull it off. Here comes the cake. A Queen of Sheba. No Queen of Sheba for Angelo, he doesn't like sugar, good sign, he's having more cheese, Roquefort, can't find a more virile cheese than that. Reich is a genius and Freud is a little twerp. I never would have thought Aunt Ro read anything else but *Better Homes and Gardens*. Ro, this famous Reich, and Abel, a superb trinity. Based on that, we'll be zipping off to Italy in no time flat.

A sexually healthy person must stop being unconsciously hypocritical to become so consciously in regard to the social institutions that prevent the development of a natural healthy sexuality, Abel intones while pouring himself champagne. Bravo, some Queen of Sheba to celebrate that, and some Dom Perignon, just a little more. And on it goes. What a memory that Abel has. But clever people are those who modify their entourage in such a way as to eradicate the frustrating effect of the social order. Their entourage, obviously, Saint-Germain or the Tabac des Folies, you can't really call them a gulag. Mmm . . . *patriarchal culture . . . the physical structure of the masses . . . the fantasies of murdering the father . . .* —beating old people to death with telephone directories, obviously . . . *—the antisocial nature of the unconscious . . .* coffee. *The renunciation of instinct in order to adapt to social necessity . . .* no, we will not renounce. Instinct is going to Venice with Angelo. Got to blow the whole thing sky high, Abel says. First, the cork on the second bottle of bubbly. A bottle of bubbly, that's happiness. In the fizz we see a future much rosier than in broth. Only thing is it makes you want to piss. Too bad about leaving Wilhelm Reich like this, but something tells me I'll get back to him later.

To reach the garden toilets, whose wobbly door is pierced with a hole for ventilation and oglers, you take a small path to the left of the perron. A real expedition when you're a little smashed. On the way back, I come across Angelo, who plants himself in front of me leaning on one foot, then the other, with a delighted frustrated look about him. Horrible seconds of silence, which I break with a "the toilets are that way," five words ripped from the bottom of my throat which want to express everything, absolutely everything, about the importance of toilets in a person's love life; don't accuse me of being scatological, but there isn't a more classic trick in the book, what better pretext for following a girl you dare not approach in a restaurant or during a lunch like this one, than taking off after her to the john, sometimes it's called the phone, but it all comes down to the same thing, what options do you have in this castrating, patriarchal society for saying straight out to the woman of one's life, "Come on, we'll get it on right away or if not right away, a little later, give me your phone number," impossible because first of all you're afraid of being judged by others, secondly, of getting your face slapped, if you drink from the cup at least let it be in private so let's go off toward that little corner—and the lovely lady, hooked by a look, heading toward the *buen retiro* where everything can happen, nowadays Romeo and Juliet wouldn't speak to each other for the first time at a dance, meaning a chic nightclub where everybody remains aloof, because Parisian evenings are no longer adventuresome nor permissive, no passions come to a head in the place that by rights should be even more stylish than the rest, superb, with silver shells in the shape of sinks and classical music—the door of the john normally reserved for the gardener's exclusive use clacks with a sound of abandon—*have you ever traveled, Mademoiselle, on the high seas?*—on the left, thank you, the green door—mademoiselle, your eyes, mademoiselle your wide-brimmed hat and these delicious cherries and that pink dress, I don't know a thing about outfits but that one there looks so great, like you were born in it, what are you doing tonight? As if I had the choice. As if I was hesitating between a short stroll to help me digest and—and what? Valbonne, he says. Up above Cannes. A swimming pool. He insists on the swimming pool as if that was supposed to especially lure me. Even if it's a plain old puddle I'll go, Angelo, even though I hate swimming pools and midnight swims that freeze the dinner in your stomach and wreck your makeup, not to mention your hair, as for bands I'd rather have some good records and a P.A. system any day— but tonight I'll come up with a few water ballets, I'll discover some original dance figures, I'll be nothing less, so that you'll love me, than Esther Williams and Isadora Duncan wrapped up in one.

Fucking, Wilhelm Reich states in other terms, contradicts in every respect present-day laws and all patriarchal religion. THE FAMILY IS NOT THE CORNERSTONE OF SOCIETY BUT THE PRODUCT OF ITS ECONOMIC STRUCTURE, Abel bellows, deeply flushed by the Dom P. Will you stop reciting that to us by heart, Hughette says dipping a lump of sugar into her coffee, you're a pain in the ass, Abel. Don't pay him any mind, Madame, he's a little smashed. Aunt Ro, too, resting languidly on what she calls her rocker, neglects prudence to the point of removing her headgear, which gives me the chance to slip into her ear: listen Ro, all right if I go to Valbonne tonight with Angelo?

Then she smiles, her pupils not much darker than the

clear disc of her eyes, contracting like a cat's in the sunlight into narrow tapering slits—and I recognize, just by the gradual crinkling of her lips, the mute exquisite queen of the kingdom of Jawohl.

*

Aunt Ro was to take to her grave a far more serious secret, that of my going off to Venice with Angelo, without me ever knowing the deep cause for her complicity; by way of an answer, I had to make do with an imperceptible twinkle of malice under her half-closed eyelids, with her silence that burst louder than the trumpets of Jericho, and with her smile as subtle as a kore's in the Parthenon or a bodhisattva's renouncing paradise in order to stay on earth and save some troubled souls.

Aunt Ro, who had been wandering for ever so long through the corridors of her hotel looking for the ghost of herself at fifteen, had finally laid her hands on it and let it fly off toward Italy, an act of gratuitous generosity like buying birds for the single purpose of opening their cages, or an urge to take revenge on life that pushed her to slip into my bundle of belongings five bars of Tobler chocolate, a map of Italy, a thousand francs she had removed from the wad of bills that she was hiding in a Galle vase, a calendar, and an explanatory leaflet on the Ogino method whose effectiveness seemed as certain to her as the effect of the laws of gravity—what do her motivations matter, Aunt Ro thrusting out her torso like the *Victory of Samothrace* and squeezing the complete works of Wilhelm Reich under her arms, rears up in my memory like a sign, a magic stele, a road marker, indicating with the point of her umbrella the pathway of metamorphoses as Mme. Méry-Guichard had done, and Hughette and Abel who also, in their way, had helped me realize the Nietzschean ambition of every human being: to become what he or she is.

Certain images get jammed in the magic lantern, the sort that touch the subtle, essential level of ourselves, stupid images reviving an eternal present and that must be decoded like an old alphabet.

There was, on the ceiling of room 16, Hôtel Univers in Cannes, a crack, as capricious as the course of an affluent of the Casamance, whose twists and turns I loved to follow until they became a subconscious crevice enlarging to the point of bringing the ceiling down, as well as the whole sensible world. There were the washed-out shreds of light of the village of Domodossola, at the Italian border—permit to leave France? nothing to declare? How could there be nothing, when we were living the true, the sincere, the naive adventure, the wild, wild life, and that I was plunged smack in the middle of a tribal, religious, magic initiation, that I had just cut the cord linking me to the matriarchal world to take off at top speed toward the fringes of my inner frontiers, so when we were getting close to Loano where Angelo knew a *pensione* where they would put us up for nothing, doesn't that have to be declared? no tax on mental treasures, some things you just got to accept, said the customs agent while sliding the door closed.

You want me to tell you all about it, Polline, the Pensione Giulia where the owner stuffed us with green lasagna on the house, the Coppertone poster on the wall across the way, the one where the dog is pulling the little girl's trunks down, baring her pure white bottom—Coppertone, that's the most beautiful memory of my wedding night, something like the paintings at Ajanta or the frescoes at Altamira, go ahead, shrug, but tell me, Polline, what will be left of our childhood when passing time will have once and for all wiped away the Pâtes La Lune poster on its little section of gray wall, rue de Steinkerque, and after age fourteen when it will have shredded the Coppertone sign opposite the Pensione Giulia—unless a nuclear war would leave erect as menhirs and as enigmatic as the standing stones of Ireland, nothing but these two sections of wall more precious to me than the famous little yellow one sanctified by literature —what a mockery if all that was left of our superb planetary civilization when travelers from the future arrived were these four masterpieces taken out of a parody of an imaginary museum: the Pasta moon smiling ear to ear on a wall in Montmartre, the Priapus of Pompeii weighing his colossal organ upon the divine scale, the little Coppertone girl with braids, and Nut the goddess of the heavens arching her body until her toes touch her oversized fingertips, wouldn't that be better than all the libraries, this fresco glorifying food, love, the sun, and the cosmos—even though I still shed tears over the conflagration at Alexandria, it really makes me scream and shout when I think about all that lost food for the soul. All the rest, before eternity, just piffles. The thirty-year-long war in Vietnam, in relation to the history of the earth: zero. So the summer of '64, well, you can just imagine. Getting wrecked on chianti at Mario and Elena's, the Chinese lanterns at the dance trembling in the water, redder than the accordion reflection of the full moon, the palm trees of the Corso pompously called Roma so threadbare that they looked fake, the holidays of a summer when we rocked and drifted upon rivers of syrup, "Una lacrima sul viso," one hell of a mushy hit at the very sound of which I would have got it on with a legless cripple, so you can imagine the ecstasy I was in with Angelo—not a damn thing in comparison to the distance separating the stars. So I dance at the huge Paradiso while Johnny Halliday sings "Retiens la nuit" and now wings go growing on me as on fireflies, with a flick of my nail I peel off the placental film masking my true face, I have achieved my nymphal molting, proof of which is my lip bitten and swollen with an initiatory scar.

*

Divirginizing me really bugged the hell out of Angelo; the guy had laid so many broads without loving them and here he wanted to treat himself to the luxury of a platonic love—I was apprehensive, after six months of prison, come on, but no, he told me, I screwed a slut in Cannes, it can wait, you're something else, for you I got to come up with something special—you see I don't give a damn about coming, there are so so many sluts, cunts, holes, what a nightmare when I get to thinking about it, the whole mess dangling down pathetically, now you at the very limit, you've got the sex the angels have, you wouldn't by any chance be an optical illusion, do people fuck princesses who step out of cartoons, with sparrows carrying their trains in their beaks, I don't dare, you see, I don't dare, I get the impression that if I touch you you'll go up in smoke, or change into a marble statue at the back of some Italian garden—now in a certain sense I felt flattered, in another I would have preferred to get it over and done with right away but after all it was up to him to decide, as a matter of fact I think he was scared to death because he had never seen a virgin up close before, besides his sisters, and that wasn't yesterday.

I would like to tell you, Polline, about the pink and ocher houses sunlit with flaking makeup, the sordid quality of the South, its decrepit look, its filthy feverish charm like a fifteen-year-old whore's in a suburb of Naples, the Italy that's all for show, a put-on, all old-time seasoned culture, made up of shouting and colors, about the *naytt cloobs,* the Frantonio, the Marinella, the Fontanella, the convertibles of the rich brats of Turin and Milan that accelerated at the cop's whistles, whose dagos are macho as hell, with their shirts open on their hairy torsos, a real carpet, a big gold chain buried deep down, and their hair reeking of anti-dandruff lotion. And the train. Sneaking into the Loano-Genoa local, crammed with fat mammas, bawling kids and men in shirt sleeves, the corridors we charged down, the conductor on our tails, slipping on fruit peels and Motta ice-cream wrappers—and Genoa, the street of the whores where drunken sailors wobbled along, the room we rented at a washerwoman's who dealt in illegal pullovers, the sheets stinking of cheap bleach, the kind that burns your hands, the cemetery where we looked for Marco Polo's tomb, the alleyways, just wide enough to hang two pair of undershorts out to dry on a rope stretched from one window to the other, the combat ground of cats and rats, unable to tell one from the other, given the scrawniness of the first and the obesity of the latter, and then the highway.

The *autostrada.* Another story. In '64 the mad rush hadn't started yet. The only hitchhikers you saw were old hands at it. Professional hoboes. We had a slightly amateur air about us, but it worked out, we even got offers for meals in chic trattorias by the dagos who were hoping to lay me after dessert—*e la mia sorella,* Angelo said, directing a cannibal smile toward the trick who cleared off pronto, the dagos come off like that, Angelo said, shoot their mouths off and all that, but they're stuffed with starch, mushy balls and all that, digesting all day long, it's soft as marshmallow, an English thing that sticks in your teeth. I ate some when I was in Liverpool, two years ago, you don't know what it was like, did we ever let them have it on the beaches, those Mods and Rockers, man oh man.

Excuse me, Polline interrupts, but I think your guy is fantasizing. As far as letting them have it, the French were the ones on the receiving end, and the punitive expeditions to Great Britain often wound up with our guys in the hospital—but anyway, go on. Talk to me about hunting the fags who hid out in the beach huts at Loano to get sucked off by little boys . . .

Oh yeah, we met a whole group of guys from the Drugstore also on vacation, who spent their nights taking off after queens on the beach, stripping them naked and dunking them in the water until they were half-drowned—genuine faggot raids, you had to see the mob of stark naked guys all running a cross-country, elbows hugging their bodies, along the waves, pursued by the gang armed with sticks yanked off of the lounge chairs—I didn't participate myself, I just watched, but Angelo went right at it, motivated by a merciless hatred toward fags that would have driven him to finish them off if he hadn't been neutralized in time.

And the day when the black limo gave us a lift. . . . Neat-looking hearse, with a stiff's skull and crossbones painted on the front of the body. Shall we take it? Angelo asks. You don't hitchhike with death, I said, pale with fright. You'll see if you don't, Angelo said, after two hours standing here freezing on the edge of this highway. The driver opened the door for us, he drove on without a word, without turning around, like a madman, and I kept my eyes closed sure we were going to smash up—well, as it turned out, we didn't, we got out in one piece, death watched us through the rearview mirror, disheartened by our prodigiously naive and seraphic appearance, he cast us out on the shoulder so that we wouldn't go spreading our subversive example of happiness down in hell.

And the cat story—a beige cat found in the Bologna train station, clodhopper capital, shoes I mean, that's all there is in that city, not the least aesthetic interest, nothing but tanned meat in all its forms, so this cat had the runs, no way of keeping him but how sad we were when we had to abandon it. And the plaster Venus that Angelo had stolen in a garden, convinced he had laid hands on an original excavated from a site at the Acropolis, and the milk trucks plundered at dawn, and the maniac truck driver . . .

Listen up a second to the truck driver story. We stop a truck, still on the highway, I stretch out on the back seat, Angelo sits up front on the driver's left, and I start snoozing; disturbed by a rubbing around my fly, I open an eye and discover the hallucinated profile of the driver who was in the middle of fiddling at my zipper with his free hand. Now I say to myself: he mustn't have gotten laid for two weeks, it's enough to make you gaga, all this cutting back and forth across the highway by yourself—an endless interplay then follows between me curled into a ball and his stubborn, insightful fingers, animated by a sort of personal genius that lent them a fearsome agility. I hit Angelo all I could, impossible to wake him up, when a guy nineteen is asleep he's in a coma, meanwhile the trucker is barreling ahead like a lunatic clinging to the wheel with one hand and with the other pursuing his exploration, nothing is working, neither insults nor swift kicks, I'd gladly gouge his eyes out with my dago penknife if I wasn't sure we'd wind up with our wheels in the air in some ditch—when we get to Venice—Venezia

10 Miles—this suburb's really something, crammed with
factories plus in August the weather's horrendous, the
truck brakes, the pithecanthrope wakes Angelo up with an
elbow jab, what am I saying, with a flick of his fingers, you
have to believe the kid had gotten his zzz's in to his heart's
content, the bum, I pry myself out black and blue and slip
like a rag between his paws—what's with you, he says,
you're all pale, didn't you get any sleep?

You see, Polline, first off I got scared—I thought we'd never get out of that cursed city alive, where the labyrinths of the canals open only onto dead ends or closed-off squares, and that it would hold us in its shadowy forest of rib vaults, the Dogaressa, until one false move brought us to the bottom of some lead-roofed dungeon where the skeletons of con-spirators whose names are now forgotten are crumbling to dust, I thought we would not escape the traps of the old pythoness who knows the tales of the Orient, the leonine woman, the decayed lady, the pock-marked creature, the cancerous Serenissima, the lagoon Republic of the sewers, the queen of a royal hive with complicated cells where the golden honey of illuminations is drying—and then she made herself into a courtesan with porphyry fingers to dazzle us with her costume balls and her Turkish tricks, to please us she took out her old flashy festival rags and revived the ghost of Theodora come from a blood Mass—there she goes passing under the porchway of San Marco in her palanquin chiseled with the dry splatter of pigeon droppings, hoist me on your shoulders Angelo so I can see, between the torn curtains she parts with her gold-laden fingers, as heavy as a dream of Byzantine autumn, the cruel icon, cheeks painted with red chalk, draped in her brocades the color of agony, scarcely more artificial than those of the city walls, scoured and drunk down by time, a palette of pearl, of rust, of strawberry and sherbet, acidic and grating like the wind gusting in from the sea, fresh and raw like a page from the *Shah-nama* or a missal upon which ink and crushed precious stones have finally taken on their definitive hues, tarnished only by a chiaroscuro of soot on the facade of the Libreria, or the mark of a sorcerer's black fingers fading with anthracite the arcades of the old Procuratorships, the Romanesque rose windows, the carnivorous convolvulus of the balconies and the trellis of the *moucharebiehs*.

Don't let go of my hand Angelo, or else the poison lady will separate us, I'm as wary of her as the black plague, especially that time of day when in the canals vermilion reflections tremble like blood smears, the twilight hour when she becomes Greek, Persian and Chinese, as inscrutable as Carapaccio's *Courtesans,* a painting without a backdrop, a Siena-blue clot of coagulated time, before which we stood fascinated, focusing on the folds of silk, the fur of the dogs, the sparkle of the jewels against the skin, until we make out, our heads spinning as if we had chewed on peyote leaves, the secret essence of pictural matter, and beyond, the seed of existence, the unfiltered Body of Buddha and eternity projected upon a surface arbitrarily circumscribed by a golden frame.

Who still knows the Courtesans' absent-minded games, who knows toward what other land they direct their gaze, touched by a pearly ennui—is it already toward the Bosphorus and the Sea of Marmara, or only toward Torcello, the first island where the future builders of Venice sought refuge, chased by the barbarian invasion, Torcello pearl of the lagoon, the guide says, surrounded like Saturn with a ring of mist from which the ferryman looms in his beribboned boater, vanishing point of the truncated perspectives of the dream, Cythera and Avalon where everything begins

and ends with the echo of the baptistry bells, a land of
swamps from which wild geese take flight, crying out in a
milky sky that is so autumnal you are surprised that the vine-
yards are not yet red.

*

At the Florian café the orchestra della Municipalitè e dei
Poveri always played the same waltz while all around us the
Western World rotted away and the century teetered into
its last quarter—in a few years would be born the pathetic
dawn of one certain black spring, there would be Woodstock and thousands of kids on the road, but while I was
looking at the reflection of Venice in the lagoon I was
already seeing the minarets of Istanbul tremble and I knew I
had done with the age of metamorphoses—Angelo had
taught me the secret language of the mystery cults, I had
slipped while crawling into the cave of the Pythian
Prophetess awaiting me with backside planted on her
tripod, breathing in from below a good dose of dry leaves,
before regurgitating a bit of my destiny in a belch of shimmering snot; I had dived into the baths of herbs and blood,
resolved the enigma of my past by giving the Sphinx a run
for its money and knocked over the chariot of good old
Laius on the road to Venice, I knew how to walk on fire and
swim under ice, the spirits had stuffed my belly with magic
quartz in place of my bowels and removed my brain so that
I'd forget I had been taught to talk and to laugh like other
people, never again would I return to the fold of women
who wailed out their sorrow about having lost me forever as
they doused their heads with ashes—never again would I
recognize the house of my father.